I0573218

D.C. Street Savagez 2:
Bloody Massacre

By

Seth Holmes

Cadmus Publishing
www.cadmuspublishing.com

Copyright © 2022 Seth Holmes

Published by Cadmus Publishing
www.cadmuspublishing.com
Port Angeles, WA

ISBN: 978-1-63751-212-8

All rights reserved. Copyright under Berne Copyright Convention, Universal Copyright Convention, and Pan-American Copyright Convention. No part of this book may be reproduced, stored in a retrieval system, or transmitted in any form, or by any means, electronic, mechanical, photocopying, recording or otherwise, without prior permission of the author.

This is a work of fiction; therefore, names, characters, places, and incidents are the products of the author's imagination or are used fictitiously. Any resemblance to actual events, locales, or persons, living or dead, is entirely coincidental.

First, I would like to thank Frank Reuter and the whole Cadmus Publishing team for helping me get this project typed up.

To my mother Queen C, I love you and miss you so much.

To my crazy, bipolar sis Paris, Shakira, Aunt Susan Perry and God-mother Kia, thank y'all for y'all support I would've struggled with getting my first book published. Thank you, and I love you so much.

To my Grandmother Ms. Gladys, I love you and need for you to stay strong and healthy. I can't wait to have some of your cooking and banana pudding again.

To all of my cousins, aunts, uncles, nephews, and nieces, I love you and will be home soon!

To the whole fucking mob, Barbeast, Lil Mike, Boo Boo, Tuff Slim, PO, Quiet Storm, Rotnot, Slick, what's up? Keep y'all head up and continue to hold it down. Free da mob!

To all of my good men who stayed solid and didn't fold, I salute y'all a thousand times. Block MLK, Block 1st N-O, Dan 1st No, Kellz CP, Sykey from the farms, Diggs, Tay Rittenhouse, Lil Mook, J-Dub 4st, Dale 24th Bang Bang, Boosie LH, Jim-Bob, Baby Ark, Skeet from Detroit, Chattown Brown, Geno 704, 2T NC, Lil E 704, Fatts Sursum Cordas, Dirty Sursum Cordas, Live Queens NY, D46th, Bigcool, D-Lo, Pa-Pa, Teedy, Arkhead CP, Lil Kyle Ohio, Nico, Teflon, Jimmy, Fat Ty 23rd, Whimp, Kendog 21st, H-Mob, Ton, Cuz Nuno, By, Keith A, Mike Mike, Floyd 3rd, Skinny Moe, Sy Kwa.

To my brothers Todd, Beefy, Jai, and Barbeast, I'm my brother's keeper!

To Bucky Fields, we have to do a project together, big homie. Keep your head up and keep grinding, Slim.

R.I.P. to Loc Da Mayor, Brinks Truck, LBJ, Lil A, Kevo, Lil Lonnie, Sweet P, Rego, Gadget, Vedo, Kevo, Keosha, Fabo, Drevon, Ronnie Glock, Bag, Debo Goat, Butta Rockz, Fat John, Chuck, Ralph 53rd, Midnight, Black Sean, Reek, Jody Breeze, Cliff, Fat Lo, Big Todd, Neff, Uncle Tim, Aunt Bob, Snoop, Benladden, Baby Jai, Steve, Big Redds, MS Sharon, Bink, Bucket, Bo, Marcus, Miss Greta Gause, and Racer and Tim. R.I.P.!

LET'S GET IT!

DEDICATIONS

This book is dedicated to my deceased brothers Ronnie Eaton and D. Procter. Rest in peace, Glock and Bag. This one is for y'all!

Contents

CHAPTER 1

DC JAIL

It was a busy day for Correctional Officers in R&D (Receiving And Discharge) over at D.C. jail. The last bus of court returns, and new arrivals had just come in. R&D was packed with men of all kinds of different races and shapes, and sizes. After being separated from Savage and Bad-Ass, Reckless Slim was placed into a holding cell with other new arrivals. The minute Reckless Slim stepped into the holding tank he felt his stomach starting to turn. The cell smelled like shit, piss, stale bologna sandwiches and ass. Then, most of the men inside of the holding tank looked like homeless cavemen or dirty ass dope fiends.

This can't be life! They should've locked some of these mu-fuckas up in a zoo somewhere. Because these mufuckas damn sure look like animals and smelled like animals, thought Reckless Slim. He walked to the back of the holding cell and found a spot in the corner to chill and think until the officers called his name to be processed.

Once Reckless Slim got comfortable he started looking around at his new surroundings to see if he recognized any of the men from off the streets. As he studied every face in the holding cell he realized that he didn't recognize any of the men. What caught his attention was the man on the opposite side of the holding cell in the corner. The man was peeking, with his head down.

Reckless Slim thought that his eyes was playing tricks on him, until he got a good clean view of the man's face. "Damn, Mike what's up my nigga? Why you sitting there looking like you see a ghost or something? I guess my face was the last face you expected to see, Huh?" asked Reckless Slim while walking towards a scared Dope fiend Mike. Before Dope fiend Mike could reply Reckless Slim charged him, then started giving him an ass whooping that he would never forget.

"Why did you rent me a stolen car bitch?" asked Reckless Slim, delivering punch after punch. "Because of your dope fiend ass I'm in this shit hole for the rest of my life!" Reckless Slim's chest heaved in and out while continuing his brutal assault on Dope fiend Mike. By now Reckless Slim was in a rage as he crushed Dope fiend Mike's head with his fist like he was a human punching bag.

Dope fiend Mike's skeleton-like frame didn't stand a chance with Reckless Slim's powerful blows. Instead of fighting back and trying to defend himself, he just balled up in a fetal position and started screaming and yelling for help. Dope fiend Mike's screams sounded like a lil bitch and caught the attention of a C.O. passing by doing his security check rounds. After a quick peek into the holding cell the C.O. sprung into action by hitting the deuces and spraying his pepper spray into the tray slot of the holding cell.

Inmates started coughing immediately as they rushed out of the holding cell when the cell door slid open. They were holding their shirts over their mouths and noses to block out the pepper spray from making them gag and choke. Reckless Slim didn't seem fazed by the pepper spray as he was now stomping and kicking Dope fiend Mike in the head. After the deuces went off officers responded to R&D in less than thirty seconds.

It took damn near five officers to yank Reckless Slim away from Dope fiend Mike's bloody unconscious body. After being restrained, Reckless Slim was taken to the hole.

Savage watched Reckless Slim being drug to the hole through the small window in his cell door. Not too long after Reckless Slim was escorted out of R&D, a team of D.C. jail medical staff rushed into R&D then came out of the holding cell with a savagely beaten blood-dripping man on a blue stretcher. Savage stood there wondering what had transpired with Reckless Slim and the injured man. To him it seemed like everything happened in a blink of an eye. He and Reckless Slim was just on the court bus talking about Streetz, Savage's little brother. Savage knew that Reckless Slim was burnt out and a work horse just by reading Reckless Slim's case in the newspaper but, he didn't expect for him to crash out before being processed.

After count cleared, Savage went back to his unit while Bad-Ass sat in a holding cell stressing, knocked out. For a few hours he waited for an escort to take him back across the catwalk to the juvenile block.

CHAPTER 2

U.S. PENITENTIARY LEE COUNTY

Stink just received his date back for his halfway house. After seeing his case manager Stink went to his cell to change into his workout clothes. Stink started working out once he got two years short to his release date. 'Time flies by,' thought Stink as he realized that his three-year sentence was almost over. After Stink changed into his workout clothes, he grabbed his MP3 player then went to his spot in the back of the unit and started getting his workout in.

Stink's workout was called the Heart Busser and was a hell of a workout. The Heart Busser was twenty Four Pump Burpees, twenty Three pump crawl outs, twenty Mike Tyson push-up's, twenty Toe touches, twenty Spiderman push-ups, one hundred mountain climbers, twenty-five diamond push-ups, twenty-five wide push-ups, and fifty squats. Stink was in his zone while listening to Kevin Gates – Push it. And was pushing his workout to the limit. Stink was on his third set, which was the twenty Three pump crawl outs, when the two Correctional Officers that were working the unit announced an immediate lock down.

After the Correctional Officer announced the immediate lock down, Stink dropped down did five more crawl outs then grabbed his water bottle and made his way to his cell. Stink was used to being on lock down. It was times that USP Lee was on lock down for months, so Stink wasn't tripping. By now Stink was used to lock downs at USP Lee County. After Stink locked in his cell he grabbed a pair of boxer briefs, a towel, wash cloth and two soap dishes of out his locker then put a bed sheet up that him and his celly use as a curtain while taking a shit or bird bath. After Stink washed up good, he pulled his stinger out from under the bed then boiled some hot water for his Oatmeal.

"This bitch stay on lock down," said H-Mob, Stink's celly as he set on his bunk reading SOUTHEAST TRENCHES By Seth Holmes.

"I'm already hip slim but come and watch the door for me while I call Ma dukes right quick," said Stink as he went into his locker and pulled out a small black Android phone.

After Stink called his mother Ms. Carolyn, he then passed the phone to H-Mob and let him burn for a while. While Stink was eating his bowl of Oatmeal, he was thinking about the conversation that he and his mother Ms. Carolyn just had about Streetz, Stink's little brother. After hearing about Streetz arrest Stink told their mother the good news about him coming home soon. Ain't this a bitch! I'm on my way home and lil bra just coming in thought Stink.

"Aye H-Mob, after you finish on the horn, I'm going to go head and roll us up one," said Stink as he grabbed a homemade oil burner and dropped a couple of drops of Jimmy Choo Blue Fragrance Oil into the oil burner. Once Stink got the oil burner ready, he pulled out a small balloon that was packed with Sour Diesel. Stink then grabbed some toilet tissue wrapper paper and rolled up a jail house sized blunt.

When Stink made a wick to use as a lighter then fired the jail house-sized blunt up, H-Mob placed a towel below the door where the gap was at to keep the strong odor of Sour Diesel from circulating into the Unit.

"On Snoop that diesel smell good is shit moe. I'm high already and I didn't even hit it yet," said H-Mob while waiting on his turn to hit the pencil size blunt of Sour Diesel.

"Yea moe! This that pressure. I got this from the homie Glocko in B-Unit," said Stink while referring to the Sour Diesel and extending his arm out to H-Mob to pass him the blunt. Once H-Mob got the blunt he took two long pulls then started coughing and choking like he had virgin lungs.

"Damn slim is you ok? Pass that shit," said Stink as he grabbed the blunt from H-Mob and took a nice long pull before putting it out.

"Why you put it out moe?" asked H-Mob when he saw Stink put the blunt out.

"Because nigga it looked like you was about to go out for the count," replied Stink as he looked out the window at the compound.

"Shit I was about to go out. I slept on that diesel and didn't know that it hit hard like that, but bra let's hook up. I got the munchies," said H-Mob as his high kicked in.

"Say no more! I'm with that bra," replied Stink.

After Stink and H-Mob made their rice bowls they played chess for push-ups. H-Mob was up 3-2 and had Stink doing push-ups back-to-back.

"You got it bra. Fucking with you I'm going have to take another bird bath," said Stink while jumping to his feet and doing a set of twenty-five push-up's. Stink then grabbed some tissue; an AA battery and a strip of foil then made another wick and fired the blunt of Sour Diesel back up. When Stink took a few pulls then handed the blunt to H-Mob he handled the Sour Diesel like a champ and got his face back. Minutes later after the blunt was gone the Correctional Officers announced that it was count time.

After the Correctional Officers did their count, H-Mob got in his rack and went to sleep while stink pulled his phone out and called his Man's Fat Yee from down the farms. After Stink told Fat Yee his up-and-coming release date, he then told him to get a fresh outfit of the newest designer clothes with a pair of designer shoes.

Once Stink hung up the phone, he put the phone back up, brushed his teeth then hit the rack. H-Mob was already sleep and snoring. It's almost over Ma, I will be home soon thought Stink as he drifted off to sleep.

CHAPTER 3

REVENGE IS OURS

Jim-Bob and Lil E was riding all through Southeast searching for Menace, but couldn't seem to find him. They hit hood after hood, but came up short. After hearing about Streetz arrest and Cash's death, Jim-Bob and Lil E felt like it was time for them to assist Streetz. With Lil Luvah dead and Streetz, Reckless Slim and Block locked up it was nobody on the streets to retaliate against Menace for killing Cash. When Jim-Bob and Lil E pulled up around Lench Mob in the alley the spotted Pickles and Pa-Pa sitting on a porch cooling. When Jim-Bob let the driver side window down Pickles and Pa-Pa went to reaching for their waistlines.

"Y'all right here bullshitting! If I was here to spin y'all would've been dead by now. What y'all forgetting that this is the Southside? Before I even got a chance to drop my window y'all was already supposed to be filling this bitch up with lead, but look doe I need to get in y'all ear right quick. So come and take a ride with me," said Jim-Bob as he hit the locks for Pa-Pa and Pickles to get in. Once Pickles and Pa-Pa got into the Range with Jim-Bob and Lil E, Jim-Bob pulled off.

"Aye Bob, this Range Cool is shit, but too bad this bitch was about to get fucked up and Swiss cheesed! You know you can't be pulling up dropping windows in the alley like that," said Pickles while looking around in the Range checking out the interior.

"Oh yea Swiss cheesed huh? Well Pickles great minds think alike because that's exactly what me and Lil E is here to talk to you and Pa-Pa about. Don't y'all know that lil situation that happened with my man's Streetz lil man's, Lil Luvah a few months ago?" asked Jim-Bob.

"Yea we remember. Matter fact you we was just talking about that shit. You talking about the lil dude Lil Luvah that killed Menace brother Domo right?" replied Pa-Pa.

"Yea Slim we on the same page! Anyways, me and Lil E been riding around looking for this nigga, but we can't seem to find him.

Word on the streets is that slim is going around bragging about killing Streetz right hand man's Cash, and with Streetz, Block and Reckless Slim lunching ass being locked up it's nobody here to Swiss cheese Menace, but me and Lil E, so I need for y'all to keep y'all ears and eyes open. The minute y'all see Menace or hear about his where abouts call me A.S.A.P," said Jim-Bob while handing Pickles a napkin with his number on it.

"Say no more! Now drop us back off around the mob. It was just cranking like shit out there and it ain't no telling how many sells we done missed," said Pickles while thinking about all of the money he was missing. After Jim-Bob dropped Pickles and Pa-Pa off, him and Lil E then made their way around Congress Park.

"Aye bob do you really think that we can trust them niggas? I mean what if they try to get us backed doored or something?" asked Lil E while trying to figure out Pickles and Pa-Pa out.

"Bra, Pa-Pa and Pickles are some stand up niggas. Now do I trust them 100 percent? Fuck No! But what I do trust is that they would call me as soon as they see Menace or hear about his whereabouts." Replied Jim-Bob.

Hours Later

Pickles was sitting on the front porch catching sales after sales when he noticed Menace pull up in the alley in his smoke gray Dodge Challenger and park. Pickles immediately pulled out his phone and shot Jim-Bob a text message telling him that Menace just pulled up around Lench Mob in the alley. Jim-Bob shot back and told Pickles that him and Lil E was on the way and to keep Menace around until they got there. After Menace parked his Dodge Challenger he got out and walked up on the porch and set with Pickles. By now Pa-Pa was back. He was just coming out of the trap with Old Face's big booty ass. She just put that fire head on Pa-Pa. Old Face was a dog with her head game and just like a dog she just ate, sucked and licked the meat off the bone.

"Pickles what's up moe? I didn't know that Pa-Pa was fucking with Old Face," said Menace when Pa-Pa and Old Face came out the trap and walked right past him without speaking to him.

"Yea bra be slutting her out catching the head here and there, but what's up with you doe?" asked Pickles.

"Shit just cooling, do you got some weed on you?"

"Come on slim, that's like asking a farmer is a pig pork! You know I stay with that pressure," replied Pickles.

"Say no more! Let me get a ounce up off you then," said Menace while pulling out a small bank roll and pulling two blue face hundred dollar bills and a fifty.

"Hold up for a second bra. I have to step in the trap and grab it for you. I only got Michael Vick's on me," replied Pickles as he stood up from out of the chair.

"Cool, I'm going to be right here waiting, but don't keep me waiting too long because I haven't smoked all day," said Menace.

"Aite bet," replied Pickles as he went inside the trap to get a ounce of OG Purp. When Pickles got inside the trap he pulled his phone back out and shot Jim-Bob a text that said – "HURRY UP!"

Jim-Bob shot back and said, "Already here slim. Make sure you are out of the gun line. Me and Lil E is coming off of the back street now. Where is slim at?" asked Jim-bob.

"He's out front sitting on the porch," replied Pickles.

"Cool!" Texted back Jim-Bob.

"Aye E keep the truck running. Once you hear the shots go off meet me at the corner," said Jim-Bob while sliding one in the head of his fully Mac 10 .45.

"Aite Bob I got you! But I'm telling you now and again that I don't trust Pickles and Pa-Pa. If you not back in less than 45 seconds then I'm coming around that corner with this here choppa cutting everything down that I see in my sight," said Lil E while reaching in the back seat and grabbing hold of a one hundred shot choppa.

"Be cool bra. Shit is about to get real. I'm just doing what I know Streetz would have done for me," replied Jim-Bob while tucking the fully Mac 10 .45 and jumping out of the Range. A few minutes later Pickles returned with the ounce and handed Menace the product. Menace gave Pickles the money for the ounce then started inspecting it. After Menace inspected the ounce he then pulled out some bamboo sheets and funnel.

Menace filled the bamboo sheet up with a gram of OG Purp then spiked it with a pinch of funnel. Once the OG Purp was rolled up Menace then pulled out a Bic lighter and put that shit in the air. Menace took four nice pulls of the OG Purp then passed it to Pickles. Just as Pickles extended his arm out to grab the OG Purp Jim-Bob spent the bin and put a red beam on the back of Menace's head. Menace saw the confused look in Pickles' eyes and wondered what had just caught Pickles' attention, so he decided to follow Pickles' eyes and try to turn around, but before he got a chance to turn around Jim-Bob pulled the trigger two times. Boc! Boc! Menace's head split open like a banana leaving brains and blood everywhere. After Menace's dead corpse dropped to the ground Jim-Bob ran up and put five more in him. Boc! Boc! Boc! Boc! Boc!

"Streetz sends his love. Come on Pickles we have to get the fuck out of here. I know you hear them sirens," said Jim-Bob while pulling Pickles along with him.

After Jim-Bob and Pickles made it to the Range they got in then Lil E pulled off. While driving Lil E kept making eye contact with Pickles through the rear-view mirror. It was just something that Lil E didn't like about Pickles. All three men drove in complete silence as Lil E drove the Range through Anacostia Park. Lil E found a parking spot near the train tracks and rail roads then parked and let Jim-Bob out for he can toss his murder weapon into the Anacostia River. When Jim-Bob got back into the Range, Lil E spoke and said, "Bob you drive. I got to take a piss right quick."

"Cool! Aye Pickles come and ride shotgun bra," Replied Jim-Bob as he patted the passenger seat with his right hand. When Lil E saw Pickles get out the back seat and get into the front seat, he put his dick back into his pants then made his way back to the Range. When Lil E got into the back seat behind Pickles, Jim-Bob looked in the rear view mirror and gave him a head nod. Boom! Boom!

"I didn't trust that nigga anyway! Now help me toss his ass into the river," said Lil E as he got out of the back seat, opened the passenger side door then started dragging Pickles' corpse towards the river.

"Damn E, I kind of like Pickles, but too bad that he didn't see the back door coming huh," said Jim-Bob after they tossed Pickles' corpse into the river.

"Man fuck all that! He probably would've tried to back door us if he got the chance. Now let's go get the Range detailed then go get us some pussy," said Lil E.

"Cool," replied Jim-Bob.

CHAPTER 4

MEKA

After being in labor for four hours Meka finally gave birth to a healthy lil boy. The boy was a spitting image of his father, and Meka named him Trevon Luvah Johnson. Ms. Brenda, Lil Luvah's mother was in tears as she held and rocked her first grandbaby back and forth.

"Child, he looks just like his daddy. If my Trevon was here he would've been so proud and happy," said Ms. Brenda as she continued to rock a sleeping baby Trevon back and forth.

"I know Ms. Brenda. He does look like his daddy, but maybe that's only because I thought about Luvah- I mean Trevon my whole pregnancy," replied Meka while hitting the switches on the side of the hospital bed to sit up some.

"Well child let's be happy that Trevon still has a part of him here with us. I'm so happy that you got in contact with me. Now here take your son while I got get us something to eat. I know you hungry," said Ms. Brenda while handing Meka baby Trevon.

Meka laid baby Trevon on her chest then turned on the TV and started flicking through the channels. Fox 5 was reporting live from around Woodland Terrace apartments A.K.A Lench Mob. Meka didn't catch the beginning of the news, but from what the anchorman from Fox 5 News was saying Meka could tell that somebody had gotten killed, but the police had no leads or suspects in the killing. Just another unsolved murder in the hood, thought Meka as she kissed her son on his tiny little curly head.

"Welcome to this cold dark world son. I'm going to protect you and love you no matter what. I promise to keep you away from all evil. I just wish that your father was here with us," said Meka while playing with baby Trevon's curly hair.

"Child I started to get us some pizza from the hospital cafeteria, but I changed my mind and got us some Panera bread," said Ms. Brenda as she entered Meka's room and handed her a grilled chicken salad.

"Thank you Ms. Brenda. This salad looks delicious," replied Meka as she inspected her grilled chicken salad.

"No problem baby! Now sit that baby down for you can eat," said Ms. Brenda.

After Meka finished eating her salad, Ms. Brenda told her story after story about Trevon A.K.A Lil Luvah. By the time Ms. Brenda was finished Meka was in tears. And even doe Meka knew that her and Lil Luvah only fucked a few times and wasn't in a full relationship Meka now felt like she knew Lil Luvah her whole life.

Ms. Brenda told Meka stories about Trevon from when he was just a little boy all the way up until he was in high school. After hearing about how Lil Luvah use to piss the bed, Meka looked over at her son then prayed that he don't piss the bed.

"Ms. Brenda I have a few things that I would like to share with you as well," said Meka.

"Ok baby. What is it that you want to share with me?" asked

Ms. Brenda.

"Well first I want to tell you a little about myself. Then I'm going to tell you my plans for me and baby Trevon," replied Meka while closing the lid on her container and setting her salad to the side.

"Ok baby I'm listening."

"Ms. Brenda I grew up without a father as well. All me and my sisters had were each other. We didn't have much growing up. We all shared the same clothes and shoes. We even shared the same bath water sometimes because momma used to complain about not having enough money to run the water all day. Me and my two sisters, Moni and Missy grew up in a old run down apartment building in Southeast called Co-Gardens. Momma did everything she can do to raise us. But after momma got picked up by the law for trying to turn tricks, me and my sisters was taken away by Child Family Services. Ms. Brenda I'm only telling you all this because I refuse to let my son grow up struggling like me and my sisters did.

I don't want to raise my son here in D.C. I want to move my son away from all of this evil madness. I'm going to make sure my son is straight by any means necessary. I'm going to protect and love him unconditionally. But in order to do all of this, I have to take my son and move to another city or state," said Meka.

"Child from a mother's view and experience I truly understand where you coming from. Now do I like the idea of you moving away with my only grand baby? No! But baby do what you think is best for you and your son. I can't have you raising my grand baby around all of this killing that's going on, but baby let's pray and leave it all in God's hands," said Ms. Brenda.

Just as Meka and Ms. Brenda finished praying a nurse knocked on Meka's door and told Ms. Brenda that visiting hours are now over. Ms. Brenda kissed her grand baby on his forehead and then told Meka that she will be back the following day. When Ms. Brenda left Meka finished her grilled chicken salad then watched TV until she drifted off to sleep with baby Trevon in her arms.

CHAPTER 5

STREETZ

After being classified as pretrial medium, Case Manager Denton pulled some strings with the daytime O.I.C (Officer in Charge) in housing unit South-2 to let Streetz be housed in the Intake/Detail block. In Streetz' eyes being able to stay in South-2 was a come up! Streetz was in a hell of a position because he knew that all new arrivals had to come through South-2 to get classified.

Streetz had the opportunity to catch a opp, drugs and whatever else it was that came through South-2 before other inmates in the general population units. Streetz was on the top left tier doing his detail when he noticed a group of new arrivals enter the sally port. This was Streetz second week on South-2 and Streetz still haven't came across any drugs and opp or cigarettes, but today Streetz felt like it was his lucky day. When the group of new arrivals entered the unit and went to their assigned cells Streetz put his detail to the side and went to gather up a couple of his niggaz and told them what was up. Streetz had a vicious vendetta for all ratz, especially after losing his brothers and homies to the jail system because of a rat.

"Listen y'all, that nigga that just went into cell thirteen is a rat. That's the nigga Bryant that told on Boo-Boo and Tuff-Slim," said Streetz as he put his niggas Drama and Sama on point.

"Say no more! What's up?" asked Drama ready to work.

"You already know what's up. I'm about to send his hot ass to the moon," replied Streetz.

Drama and Sama both nodded in agreement then went to get their homemade shanks from out of their cells. Sama and Drama were two knuckleheads from around One Deuce that had been in and out of jail since they were juveniles.

Sama was a tall slim, brown-skinned nigga with long dreads that can dress his ass off. Drama on the other hand was a shade or two lighter than Sama with short dreads and a big ass head. After retrieving their shanks, Sama and Drama met back up with Streetz in the TV room on the top right tier. Later that day the inmates was out getting they forty-five minutes of rec time when Streetz noticed Bryant and two other dudes sitting at a table playing dominos.

After waiting patiently for about twenty minutes Streetz was now ready to make his move.

"I'm about to show y'all niggaz how to smash a rat," said Streetz with fire in his eyes and anger written all over his face. After that Streetz didn't say another word. He got up and made his way over towards Bryant.

"Master Splinter what's up slim?" asked Streetz while he tapped Bryant on his shoulder. When Bryant looked back over his shoulder Streetz pulled out his shank and plunged it into Bryant's head. Once Bryant felt the strong impact from the shank he tried to get up and run, but Streetz was all over him plunging it into Bryant's head.

Blood was squirting everywhere while Streetz was putting

his shank in Bryant hot ass. By now it was a slaughter house in South-2. Them boys was working. Sama and Drama joined in on the action and started getting their shanks bloody. They was doing their thing on the two unknown men that Bryant was playing dominos with. It wasn't that they wanted to be a part of something, they just played and lived by the rules which was – IF YOU HANG WITH A RAT YOU GET TREATED LIKE A RAT.

The officer working the control bubble was in shock as he watched Streetz, Drama and Sama put their knife game down. It took him a few seconds to get his self together before he hit the deuces and alerted all available officers to respond to housing unit South-2. Streetz was in a rage as he continued to plunge his shank in and out of Bryant.

"Because of niggaz like you," Plunge!

"It's a lot of good men in the feds," spat Streetz while still plunging his shank into Bryant. Officers started coming through the sally port blissing like N.F.L line backers. When Streetz looked up and saw all of the Correctional Officers he stabbed Bryant two more times. Plunge! Plunge! Then took off running towards his cell to go and try to flush his shank, but before he made it to his cell he was tackled to the ground by a Correctional Officer then pepper sprayed.

"Arghh shit," growled Streetz when the Correctional Officer sprayed him. Sama threw his shank in the gym while Drama followed Streetz lead and took off running towards his cell as well. It was a bloody massacre in South-2 and after restraining the men that started the bloody massacre officers had to attend to the three men that was bleeding a pool of blood and was in serious pain while feeling the life slipping out their bodies.

Streetz was taken to hole South-1 while Drama and Sama was taken to hole North-1.

Reckless Slim was in his rack laying down when a Correctional

Officer came to his cell and told him that he was about to get a celly. Reckless Slim gave the Correctional Officer a cold stare then got up.

"Listen! How many times do I have to tell you muthafuckas that I'm not taking no cellies?" asked Reckless Slim.

"I understand, but this is not my call. If it was up to me I will let you be housed all alone for the rest of your stay in the S.H.U (Special Housing Unit). But I'm not the one who calls the shots. Shit I'm tired of you beating on all of your cellies anyway, but I need for you to turn around and cuff up for me," said the Correctional Officer as he unlocked the tray slot and pulled his hand cuffs from off of his belt.

After Reckless Slim cuffed up the Correctional Officer waved to his co-worker and told him to bring the other inmate that was waiting in the holding tank to Reckless Slim cell. The Correctional Officer heard about the brutal knife attack that inmate Holmes put on up stairs in housing unit South-2 and knew that he was the perfect match for the inmate that's been beating on all of his cellies and giving the Correctional Officers that worked the S.H.U a hard time.

"I don't know son. This one seems pretty tuff. We just had to airlift a inmate to Washington Hospital Center behind his actions. Word around the jail right now is that the guy that he stabbed and attacked may not make it so you might want to play nice with this one," said the Correctional Officer with a grin on his face.

"Is that right? All that shit sound good, but to be honest with you I don't give a fuck about what slim did. All I know is that slim is not going to be in my cell after count," replied Reckless Slim.

"Ok Tuff Tony. Here he comes right now," said the Correctional Officer. When the cell door slid open Reckless Slim had to blink his eyes twice. He couldn't believe that his muthafucking dog was being put in the cell with him. Yes he was happy to see his nigga Streetz, but not like this and before the cell door slid back shut Reckless Slim smiled at the Correctional Officer then said, "You dumb fuck! This is my muthafucking dog right here and as you can see he's just as violent as me. Now uncuff me then uncuff my dog ole Streetz here, then get the fuck on somewhere before I shit your bitch ass down. Me and Streetz have some catching up to do."

"Fuck you, you young street punk. I will beat your lil ass if you try to throw some shit on me. Now bring your ass here for I can uncuff you then uncuff your dog as you say," barked the Correctional Officer as he opened the tray slot back up to uncuff Reckless Slim and Streetz.

After the Correctional Officer uncuffed Streetz and Reckless Slim, Streetz then embraced Reckless Slim with a brotherly hug.

"Man slim what the fuck is up moe? And what the fuck is you doing over here at 1901 D St?" asked Streetz.

"I was going to ask you the same thing bra, but I'm about to put you up on game right now. Do you remember the day that we was being followed?"

"Yeah I remember slim," replied Streetz.

"Well bra that wasn't the jack boys that was the feds moe. And that day when you called for the crew to meet at the spot I was picked up by the feds for driving a stolen car in a red zone-"

"Slim! What the fuck was you doing driving a stolen car?" asked Streetz as he cut Reckless Slim off while confused at the same time.

"Streetz if you let me talk then maybe I can tell you all about this stolen car and why I'm over 1901 instead of NuNu's pussy, but that's another story," said Reckless Slim as his mind flashed back to he and NuNu's fuck episode.

"Damn slim, you fucked NuNu huh? We really have some catching up to do, but first finish telling me about the feds and this whole stolen car thing," replied Streetz.

"Yeah I fucked that freak bitch! And it was good too. Far as the car I knew nuffing about it being stolen. Mike dope fiend ass rented it to me for two grams of heroin then the next thing I know I was being blissed and dragged out of the car by the feds while sitting at a red light on M.L.K Avenue. They had they police issued Glock .17's in my face and all bra. But anyway, after the feds did a search on the car they found Big Bertha under the seat then booked me and took me into custody," said Reckless Slim.

"Damn slim that's crazy," replied Streetz.

"Naw my nigga, what's crazy is what I'm about to tell you."

"I'm listening slim. You have my full attention."

"The match came back on Big Bertha saying that it was the gun used in the killing of the two police officers. So when I put two and two together, I thought about that day when I unloaded on that mini van that was following us that day. And Streetz, the detective that interrogated me kept asking me about you, but I told that cracker that I didn't know anybody named Streetz," said Reckless Slim.

"Them dick eaters just won't let a nigga live will they moe?" asked Streetz while shaking his head.

"I guess not bra, but Streetz I'm done bra. I copped out to two life sentences, they got the murder weapon, and my fingerprints was all over it, so I didn't stand a chance of beating that shit," replied Reckless Slim.

When Streetz heard the word two life sentences his jaws dropped and his mouth flew open. He couldn't believe what Reckless Slim had just told him. He was at a loss of words as he started pacing back and forth in the cell. The information that Reckless Slim just dropped on him was fucking with his mental and it was no way that he was going to let his muthafuckin dog get washed up to the fed system like that.

"Listen slim we are going to get you a lawyer and come up with a plan. Ain't no way that I'm going to let these crackers wash you up like that. I already lost too many of my brothers and homies to this fucked up system bnd I am not about to lose another brother," said Streetz.

"Damn moe! Speaking of your brothers, I ran into your brother Savage on the court bus. We was kicking it on the whole ride back to DC jail."

"Oh yeah, that's my nigga right there. I wonder what happened to his trial and what was the verdict?"

"He lost bra. He was telling me how the dude named Bat rocked the mic and did his thing on the stand."

"Damn slim, me and Block was supposed to smash that ratting bitch! And speaking of Block I need to find out what unit he's on and see what these people's are trying to charge him with."

"Hold up bra. So you telling me that Block is over this bitch too?" asked Reckless Slim with a confused look on his face.

"Yeah slim, me and Block got locked up together. We was lamping on that nigga Bat when the feds blissed us. We was supposed to make sure that he didn't make it to testify."

"Damn bra shit real," said Reckless Slim.

"Tell me about it," replied Streetz.

CHAPTER 6

PA-PA

Pa-Pa kept calling Pickles' phone, but couldn't seem to reach him. After seeing the news and hearing about the death of Menace, Pa-Pa's curiosity was getting the best of him. He was eager to know what was going on, so he decided to give Jim-Bob and Lil E a call.

When Pa-Pa dialed Jim-Bob's number and heard the operator say that Jim-Bob's number was no longer in service his street intuition kicked in. Pa-Pa knew and felt that it was some snake shit and foul play tossed in the game. After Pa-Pa put his dreads into a pony tail he then decided to ride through Congress Park to see if he can catch Jim-Bob and Lil E. while riding down Alabama Ave, Pa-Pa made up his mind and told himself that if Jim-Bob and Lil E act funny towards him then that was enough suspicion to know that they had something to do with Pickles going missing and not answering his phone.

When Pa-Pa turned on Thirteenth he headed straight to the back of the circle. As he maneuvered the 2018 AMG 63 Benz through the circle he noticed a small group of men sitting in front of one of the buildings shooting craps. Pa-Pa found a parking spot, threw the AMG in park, then grabbed his Sig .45 and slipped one in the head.

After Pa-Pa slipped one in the head, he then tucked the .45 in his waistline then exited the Benz. When Pa-Pa walked up on the front porch where the men was shooting craps at, he slapped hands with the few dudes that he knew then pulled Fat-Kat to the side for he can holla at him. Once Pa-Pa and Fat-Kat was out of ear reach from the others Pa-Pa asked Fat-Kat about Jim-Bob and Lil E, and when was the last time that he had heard from them or saw them. Pa-Pa told Fat-Kat that Jim-Bob number was disconnected and that it was urgent that he got up with he and Lil E.

Fat-Kat told Pa-Pa that he haven't saw or heard from neither Jim-Bob or Lil E, but when he do see one of them, or hear from one of them he will let them know that Pa-Pa came through looking for them.

"Good looking my nigga! Make sure that you do that," said Pa-Pa as he turned on his heels and walked back to his Benz and got in then pulled off. When Pa-Pa pulled off Fat-Kat pulled out his iPhone 11 and called Jim-Bob. Jim-Bob answered on the third ring.

"Kat what's good bob?" answered Jim-Bob.

"Shit cooling. Pa-Pa from around Lench Mob just came through the circle looking for you and Lil E."

"Oh yea? What type of car was he in?"

"He was in a black AMG Benz Bob."

"Cool good looking out bra. I'm going to be around there when the sun goes down. I'm about to shoot up KK joint to go pick up Lil E," replied Jim-Bob.

"Aite bet," said Fat-Kat before disconnecting the call.

"Aye Kat what's up moe? Fuck was that all about?" asked

Chuck while counting his new bank roll that he had just won in the dice game.

"Shit for real. Slim was asking me about Jim-Bob and Lil E. But at the same time he seemed like he was up to something," replied Fat-Kat.

"On John I was thinking the same thing when I noticed him getting out of the car. But let's just wait for Jim-Bob and Lil E to come through for we can really see what's up."

"Say no more. Now let's get back to this money. I'm trying to go to Stadium Strip Club tonight and see some ass and titties."

"Shit me and you both. I heard the broad Freaky Mek be doing some type of trick. They say she makes her pussy squirt after she drinks a bottle of water."

"Damn slim I have to sese that happen. My favorite strippers in Club Stadium is Pretty Reddz and Sue Bell. Awww man speaking of Sue Bell, she has this move on the pole where she slides down the pole upside down with one hand on the pole and her legs spread wide like a eagle. Then once her body touch the floor she does a split then start popping her pussy and making her ass cheeks jump one at a time," replied Fat-Kat while thinking about the night that Sue Bell had him memorized and pre-cumming in his Versace briefs. Pretty Reddz and Sue Bell both were bad ass females. Pretty Reddz was about five-foot six-inches and 140 pounds tatted up with a nice phat ass. Sue Bell on the other hand had the type of body that caught the attention of both genders men and women.

Sue Bell was about five-foot four inches and 135 pounds caramel complexion with a nice phat ass as well. Hands down Sue Bell was a bad bitch. The only problem was that she liked pussy and not dick. I never understand what females got out of bumping pussies when they can have a man taking complete control over their bodies slamming dick in them and fucking their brains out.

* * * * *

Block was sitting on a visit with Shay when she came out and told him that she was pregnant with his child.

"Block I'm pregnant," said Shay. Block didn't get mad after Shay told him that she was pregnant because he had a lot of love for her. But then at the same time lord knows that he does not need anymore kids because he already had a starting five.

"Listen baby girl. I have a lot of love for you and I'm with backing your play one-hundred percent, so whatever you want to do I'm with it. But I must tell you that I don't know what these peoples are going to do with me. They charged me with unlawful possession of a firearm and tampering with a federal witness," said Block while looking Shay in her eyes to see how she reacts to the information that he just dropped on her.

"Block, I didn't plan on aborting my child. I want you to know that I have your back through it all. No we not together, but baby I have a lot of love for you as well. And the way you make me feel when you beat this pussy up O.M.G," replied Shay as she started thinking about the last time her and Block fucked. She was sprung out off of the dick.

"Look Shay. As far you being here for me I'm not even going to hold you to that because I know how shit goes when a nigga is away and behind these gates and walls."

"So what are you saying Block?" asked Shay while rolling her eyes and catching an attitude.

"What I'm saying is this. If you going to be here then be here! But if you not then don't waste my time."

"I'm not into playing games Block. As you can see I'm willing to have your baby while you're behind bars. So that alone should show you how much a bitch likes you and fuck with you."

"Ok Shay. Now that we are on the same page I need for you to take care of a few things for me."

"Ok, I'm listening."

"I need for you to put some money on my account and your phone. Also I need for you to get in contact with my lawyer, his name is Pete Daniels. Telephone number is 202-520-5752 and his office location is 644 Indiana Ave N.W Washington D.C. 200024.

Can you remember all of this?"

"Yes I can remember. I have it all programmed in my head."

"Ok. Now go take care of that for me and tell Shadiamond to tell Streetz to get at me and I'm on the unit with his brother Savage."

"I got you boo. But when are you going to call me?"

"I will call you sometime later."

"Ok, be safe and I'm going to be waiting on your call Block."

"I got you baby girl. Now let me see you throw that phat ass back and forth while you walk away." Said Block as he stood up and placed the phone back on the receiver that was attached to the thick plexi glass. Shay got up and walked away making sure she put a extra bounce in her walk. She could feel Block's eyes on her, so she looked back over her shoulder and blew him a kiss.

When Block got back to his unit his plans was to go straight to his cell and clear his mind, but as soon as he entered the unit Ms. Walker called him over to the bubble where she was working. What do this black big butt bitch want with Clarence? Thought Block calling himself Clarence once again as he walked towards the bubble where Ms. Walker was. Ms. Walker A.K.A walk that walk was a cool pretty thick female Correctional Officer that turned heads wherever she worked in D.C. Jail.

She had inmates and her co-workers that liked to trick off ready to pay for the pussy. Standing at five-foot four-inches and 140 pounds with a perfect heart shaped ass and perfect tits that looks like coconuts, and pretty black skin that was the color of a Hershey bar-Dark Chocolate with a set of teeth that was whiter than a set of keys on a piano. Hands down. Ms. Walker was a sexy black thick muthafucka.

"Yeah what's up Ms. Walker?" asked Block as he approached the bubble.

"Not much Mr. Carr. I just wanted to let you know the inmate movement sheet just came in and you're going to be getting a celly," replied Ms. Walker.

"Ms. Walker I'm going to be real with you. I'm really not trying to have a celly right now. I'm trying to clear my head and get my thoughts together."

"Ok, I understand. Let me see check the computers and see what other single cells that we have open. I don't need nothing to happen to nobody on my shift. I want to go home at 3:30. I don't have time to be writing no extra paperwork all because of you fuck around and fuck up your celly after you done already told me that you didn't want no celly and wanted to clear your mind," said Ms. Walker while playing with the keys on the keyboard.

An inmate that was in Number four cell flicking the lights on and off caught Ms. Walker's attention. When she looked up from the computer and at Number four cell she noticed that the inmate had his dick in his hands stroking it back and forth through the open tray slot while holding eye contact with her.

"This lil nasty muthafucka up there flashing me and playing with his self while looking at me. Hell to the no! I'm not having this shit today, I'm tired of y'all disrespectful ass niggaz pulling y'all dicks out on me!" yelled Ms. Walker while snatching the phone off the hook and punching in a few numbers.

After she hung up the phone, she told Block that he didn't have to worry about getting a celly anymore because Number four cell was about to become open. Block nodded then made his way towards the small gym where inmates was playing a game of four on four basketball. When Block entered the gym he went and stood on the sideline and watched, Savage, Boo-Boo and two other dudes from Southeast run circles around four alias niggas in the court.

"You dick eating cum guzzling bitch. I done put this dick on you plenty of times and today you decide to get met sent to the hole!" yelled the inmate that was in Number four cell jacking his dick to Ms. Walker as three officers dragged him out of the unit escorting him to the hole by his neck. Ms. Walker shook the negative comments off then applied a coat of MAC lip gloss on her sexy full lips, then continued on with her day. She really didn't mind letting an inmate gun her down here and there because she knew that she was the shit and her body was enticing. She also know that inmates jacked off to female officers to release some stress.

Ms. Walker was from the hood and wasn't really on no hot shit. It's just that today she wasn't in the mood to see no dicks. In the meantime after the basketball game was over Savage walked up to Block and embraced him in a brotherly hug and said, "Block I been meaning to catch up with you to discuss how you and my lil brother Streetz got caught up trying to smash Bat the Rat." Savage was drenched in sweat from a hard game of four on four basketball.

"Man, Savage that shit happened so fast. It's like the nigga had eyes on him or something. As soon as me and bra was about to put our murder game down federal agents hit us from all angles. Savage all this shit happened in just a blink of an eye," said Block.

"Yea? That's some crazy shit right there. It seems like while y'all was watching him the feds was watching y'all."

"Maybe so, but I just found out that my broad Shay is pregnant."

"Congrats lil bra. Let me go ahead and hit this water. I'm going to finish chopping it up with you when I get out the shower," replied Savage as he started walking to his cell. While Savage went to shower, Block went and got on the phone. After telling Tay what his charges were Block then told Tay to put some money on his account and send him some pictures. Once the phone hung up, Block went back to finish talking to Ms. Walker big booty ass for a few minutes then went in his cell and took a nap until count time.

In the meantime, after the basketball game, Savage walked up to Block and embraced him in a brotherly hug and said, "Block, I been meant to get up with you to discuss how you and my little brother Streetz got caught up trying to smash Bat the Rat." Savage was drenched in sweat from a hard game of four-on-four basketball.

"Man, Savage, that shit happened so fast. It's like the nigga had eyes on him or something. As soon as me and bra was about to put our murder game down, federal agents hit us from all angles. Savage, all this shit happened in just a blink of an eye," said Block.

"Yeah? That's some crazy shit right there. It seems like while y'all was watching him the feds was watching you."

"Maybe so, but I just found out that my broad Shay is pregnant."

CHAPTER 7

KEEP YOUR EYES OPEN

After picking up Lil E, Jim-Bob put him on point about Pa-Pa sliding through the park looking for them.

"Bob, that nigga Pa-Pa might be a problem. We probably going have to go kill him ASAP. You already know that Pickles was his righthand man," said Lil E.

"It's no question that we got to kill Pa-Pa and get him out the way. I already feel it that he's getting suspicious of us having something to do with Pickles' absence. That's why I got in contact with my nigga Geno from the 704 Charlotte, North Carolina. I called him and placed an order of big boy pistols that we will need in order to go to war with Pa-Pa," replied Jim-Bob, while stopping at a red light on Mississippi and Trenton Place Southeast.

"Now we talking my language. You know that I love playing with 223s and that shit that holds 7.62s. Bob, I'm feeling like Lil

Boosie right now when he rapped that verse on his song "Clips and Choppers"—"I got my first choppa for a buck-50 man I wish that bitch was still with me as a juvenile I hit it by the club got at some pussy niggaz and fell in love with that choppa," replied Lil E. as he started rapping and thinking about his first time catching some action with a choppa.

"Damn Moe, you just took me back to '09. I used to stay playing that song on my iPod Touch. Better yet, let's…."

Boc! Boc! Boc! Boc! Boc! Skrtttt. Jim-Bob smashed the gas as his driver side window exploded into a million pieces. A masked gunman hanging out the passenger side window of a black car was dumping at Jim-Bob and Lil E with a 30 in his hands. Boc! Boc! Boc! Boc!

Jim-Bob got low in his seat and continued to smash the gas while Lil E came out the sunroof of the Range with two Glock 23s, .40s dumping, exchanging shots with the unknown gunmen in the black car. Boom! Boom! Boc! Boc! Boc! Boom!

"E, I'm hit, bra!" yelled Jim-Bob over the loud gunshots as he felt the burning sensation from the two bullets that crashed into his shoulder and arm. Jim-Bob almost lost control of the Range when he felt the two bullets crash into his body. When Lil E heard his brother yell and tell him that he was hit, he didn't even respond. He tightened his grip on the Glock 23s and emptied the clips on the black car and gunmen. Boom! Boom! Boom! Boom! Boom! Boom!

The driver of the black car swerved and rode up on a curb then crashed into a wall. Jim-Bob kept driving as blood ran down his arm. After bucking a right turn on Southern Avenue Southeast, Jim-Bob pushed the Range to its limit until he arrived in the parking lot of Greater Southeast Hospital. Jim-Bob let himself out the Range then told Lil E to get rid of the Range and go clean himself up. Lil E got into the driver's seat of the Range then asked his brother if he was going to be okay before pulling off. Jim-Bob replied and told his brother that he was okay and that he thinks that the bullets went in and out. Before Lil E pulled off,

Jim-Bob also told him to be ready to take the trip down to North Carolina and to go get a rental car ASAP.

"I'm on it bra. Call me as soon as you get discharged. I'm going to go park the Range in the back parking lot of the circle then have Chuck or Fat-Kat take me to Enterprise to get a rental," said Lil E before pulling off.

After Lil E pulled off in the Swiss-cheesed Range, Jim-Bob made his way to the entrance of Greater Southeast Emergency Room doors. When Jim-Bob stepped through the emergency room doors he was immediately swarmed by a team of Greater Southeast medical staff. His bloody shirt was drenched in blood and looked like it was painted on as it stuck to his skin. After being put on a stretcher, Jim-Bob was rushed to ICU to be treated for his gunshot wounds.

After the nurse cleaned Jim-Bob's gunshot wounds, she then patched him up and told him how lucky he was. She told Jim-Bob that the bullets didn't do any serious damage or hit any bones or nerves, they went in and out, but he would need a sling for the bullet that crashed into his shoulder. Once the nurse placed Jim-Bob's arm in a sling, she then handed him two pain killers and a prescription for more pain killers.

"Thanks, doc," said Jim-Bob as the nurse handed him the pain killers and the prescription.

"No problem. Now just sit tight for me, the detectives are on the way to speak with you," replied the sexy, petite, blue-eyed devil as she took her purple latex gloves off and tossed them in the small garbage can that sat in the corner on the floor. Yeah, right, thought Jim-Bob as he thought about being questioned by the detectives.

"I have to get the fuck out of here," mumbled Jim-Bob as he placed the pain killers and prescription in his pants pocket.

"What was that you said?" asked the blue-eyed devil trying to figure out what it was that Jim-Bob just mumbled under his breath.

"Huh? I didn't say anything. You must be hearing things, but can you go get me a cup of water, please? My mouth is kind of dry."

"Sure, you can have whatever it is that you want. Now, is that all that you want, because if not, you can have me as well," said the blue-eyed devil all seductively while tracing over her top lip with the tip of her tongue and placing her hands on her small hips.

Jim-Bob caught an instant erection as he thought about bending the blue-eyed devil over on the hospital bed and punishing her lil pussy. He never had sex with a white girl and wanted to see what all the hype was about. He wanted to see if all the freaky shit that he always heard that white girls liked was true. Then he thought about the detectives and being harassed and questioned, so instead of thinking with his dick head, he thought with the head on his shoulders and told himself that he needed to get as far away from Greater Southeast and the blue-eyed devil as quick as possible. After Jim-Bob shook the blue-eyed devil's flirtatious offer off, he told her that he will just take the cup of water.

"Thank you, doc, but I will just take the cup of water to go," said Jim-Bob.

"Okay, have it your way," replied the blue-eyed devil as she turned on her heels and switched out of Jim-Bob's hospital room.

Once the blue-eyed devil was gone, Jim-Bob counted to 25 then peeked his head out into the hallways to see if any police were in sight. When Jim-Bob saw that the hallways were clear of police and the blue-eyed devil, he ran down the hallway, hit the back stairway, then fled out the hospital. When Jim-Bob made it to the parking lot, he flagged down a taxicab and instructed the driver to take him straight around the park. After he paid the cabby, he pulled out his phone and shot Lil E a text telling him that everything was okay and that he was around the park. Lil E shot back and said, "Okay, my nigga. I will see you soon."

"Bet," replied Jim-Bob.

When Lil E pulled around the park, he drove straight to the back of the circle and parked the smoke-gray 2016 Nissan Altima in the back parking lot. After Lil E parked the Altima, he shot Jim-Bob a text asking, "Where you at, Jim-Bob?"

Jim-Bob shot back, "I'm in building 1313 with Chuck and Fat-Kat."

"Cool, coming right now, bra," replied Lil E as he tucked his phone and made his way towards Building 1313. When Lil E entered the 1313 building, he was taken aback by the strong aroma of OG purp that was in the air.

"Damn moe, that shit smells good as a muthafucka. Let me hit that shit," said Lil E as he extended his arm out to Fat-Kat to get ahold of the blunt.

"You didn't put in on this, mannnn," replied Fat-Kat as he swatted Lil E's arm away.

"Oh, so you got jokes now, huh? You on your smokey from the movie Friday shit, huh? Well nigga, I got jokes too. Now puff, puff, pass," Lil E said, finishing off the rest of the joke.

"Man, y'all niggaz lunching. Now Bob, do you mind telling me what the fuck happened to your arm? And why is it in a sling?" interjected Chuck as he cut Fat-Kat and Lil E off.

"Me and Lil E was sitting at a red light on Mississippi and Trenton when a car pulled up on us and got the dumping," said Jim-Bob, answering Chuck's question.

"What kind of car was it? And what color was it?" asked Fat-Kat.

"It was a black Benz," interjected Lil E.

"That was that nigga Pa-Pa, moe, that's the same black Benz that he came through earlier in," said Fat-Kat while finally passing Lil E the blunt.

"Say no more. After me and Lil E come back from down Charlotte, North Carolina, we are going to spend the bin and chop everything down in sight with these new cutters that we about to go get. Better yet, E is you ready?" asked Jim-Bob.

"I came out the womb ready," replied Lil E while inhaling a thick cloud of smoke.

"Cool, let's hit the highway then. Y'all niggaz be cool until we get back. We will be back in a couple of days," said Jim-Bob.

When Jim-Bob and Lil E hit the highway, Jim-Bob shot Geno a text telling him that he and Lil E was on the way. Three-and-a-half hours later Jim-Bob and Lil E arrived in Charlotte and went straight to their destination which was Hidden Valley off of North Tryon and Sugar Creek, the Northside Exit 41. As soon as Jim-Bob and Lil E pulled up around Hidden Valley, Jim-Bob shot Geno a text and told him that he and Lil E was out front. Five minutes later Geno came out of an old run-down building and bopped to the rented Altima.

Geno was a cool, laid back, getting-money type of nigga that always kept a fresh temp fade. He was brown-skinned, 5'6", 185 pounds. "What's up, my thugs? Welcome to my city," said Geno with excitement in his voice, all hyped up as he got into the back-seat.

"Still the same Geno. You been banging that lil my thug line shit since we first met back in 2018 in FCI Beckley," replied Jim-Bob.

"Shit thug, you already know. But what's good with my D.C. niggaz doe?"

"You already know what's up and what we on. Did you get everything that I asked for?" asked Jim-Bob while getting straight to the point and speaking for he and Lil E.

"Come on, bra. You already know that your thug came through for you, so don't even insult me like that. But is y'all niggaz ready to take a tour through my city and fuck some of these thick country bitches or what?"

"Shit, I'm down, my nigga," said Lil E. Fucking some thick, freaky, country bitches sounded like music to his ears.

"Well, that makes two of us because I'm damn sure down too. Now take us to the artillery," said Jim-Bob while rubbing his wounded arm.

"Aite my thugs, let's go. After this I'm going to take y'all to SouthPark Mall so y'all can get some fly shit to wear. We going out tonight."

"Say no more. Where are we going, my thug?" asked Jim-Bob.

"Shit thug, where we not going? But first we are going to hit the Epic Center which is downtown off of West Trade and Third Street. Thugs, the Epic Center have bars, clubs, bowling alleys, restaurants, and all other types of different shit."

"On John that shit sounds lit," said Lil E, stamping it on Fat John that died from around Congress Park they homeboy.

"Shit, it is lit, my thug. But that's not all. After we hit the Epic Center we going to hit Club Onyx off of the old Pineville Road off of the Ford. It stays open all night and it don't close until about five in the morning. That bitch is full of pill-popping, big-booty hoes, and plus you can bring your pistol in if you toating," boasted Geno while rubbing his hands together.

"That's what the fuck I'm talking about. I can't wait to fuck one of these bitches' brains out. I heard a long time ago from my old heads that Charlotte was the queen city anyway. Now, how about we go see what you got for us, thug," said Jim-Bob once again, reminding Geno about the guns.

"Thug, you burnt out. Geeking ass. But come on, follow me," replied Geno as he led Jim-Bob and Lil E into the building. When the trio stepped into the building, Geno led the way. They walked up a flight of stairs then walked down a hallway and stopped at a door that had a R.I.P. Deon Kay, Freddy Gray, Breonna Taylor, Jacob Blake, George Floyd, Tony Robinson, Dontre Hamilton, Trayvon Martin, Ernest Lacy, Sylville Smith sign on it. After Geno did his signature knock twice a short, red, thick female that resembled the ex-porn star Pinky answered the door in a laced cherry red G-string and bra, her perfectly manicured toes and feet set in a pair of red fuck-me pumps while her hands clutched a 32-shot MP5 submachine gun.

"Peaches, these are my thugs Jim-Bob and Lil E from D.C./ Drama City that I was telling you about. They are the ones that wanted that order that I was telling you about," said Geno while referring to the guns that Jim-Bob and Lil E wanted.

"Hey y'all, come on in. I was expecting y'all," replied Peaches while stepping to the side to let the trio enter her apartment. When the trio stepped into the apartment, Peaches started sizing Jim-Bob and Lil E up. She knew that Geno wouldn't bring no danger to her apartment, but she always moved with caution and stayed on point.

"So, what can I help you boys with today?" asked Peaches while shifting all of her weight to one side and placing one hand on her hip while still holding the MP5 in the other one. Damn, this lil red bitch thick as shit, thought Lil E while placing his hands in front of the crotch of his pants to hide his instant hard erection. Peaches smiled as she noticed the bulge in the crotch of Lil E's pants growing. She could tell that his dick was hard by his movement and the look on his face. It's no need of trying to hide it, baby. Let me see that dick. Shit, I might even sample it, thought Peaches as she felt her clit starting to throb and her pussy get wet.

"We want to buy some artillery like that pretty bitch you got there in your hands," said Jim-Bob while pointing to the MP5 in Peaches' hands.

"Okay, follow me to the back room, and how much was you looking forward to spending?" asked Peaches while leading the trio into the back bedroom. Her ass cheeks was all over the place as she was switching, throwing her ass left to right to entice Lil E. Her ass cheeks was moving like Jell-O the whole time and every step of the way. Wobble wobble, jiggle jiggle, that ass was all over the place, and when Peaches stopped at the room where the guns was and stood on the back of her legs and made her ass cheeks jump, Lil E said, "Lord have mercy on my soul." Got him, thought Peaches as she walked over to the bed and pulled the cover back to show Jim-Bob and Lil E what she had.

"Okay boys, I have it all. Now, what we have here is a M16 with a 100-shot drum. Over here we have a SKS, a fully Uzi, two all-black twin Dracos with green beams on them. A 50-shot Calico, two twin Kimber .45's with the plus 2 at the bottom of the clips. A Glock 23 .40 caliber with the 30, as you boys say in

D.C., and a fully Mac 10 .45," said Peaches while showing off everything that she had.

"What about that pretty bitch in your hands? Is she on the market too?" asked Jim-Bob trying to get Peaches' MP5 as well.

"Nice try baby boy, but this here is my personal. Me and ol' Mona here have a lot of history together and she's not going anywhere no time soon," said Peaches while referring to her MP5 as Mona.

"Well, what do you want for all of this?" asked Jim-Bob while inspecting one of the twin Dracos.

"I'll tell you what. Give me three thousand and your boy here for one night and how about we call it even," replied Peaches while winking her eye at Lil E.

"Shit, that's a sweet deal. It don't get no sweeter than that. Aye E, you up, bra, and you better perform well. Punish that pussy for the home team straight D.C. style," replied Jim-Bob while kissing one of the twin Dracos.

After Lil E heard Peaches' proposal he just sat there and smiled. It was no question that Peaches wanted the dick and Lil E was going to make sure that he delivered it to her on a silver platter.

"Lil E, don't be all soft and shit, my thug. I'm telling you now that Peaches likes that rough shit. She like to be twisted, tossed, and turned. She like for a nigga to take full control and give her that thug loving," said Geno while thinking back to when he sampled Peaches' Georgia peach.

After Jim-Bob and Lil E wrapped all of the guns in a bed-sheet, Jim-Bob pulled out a healthy stack, pulled off 30 blue-face Ben Franklins, then handed them to Peaches.

"Thank you, sweetie. It was nice doing business with you," said Peaches while stuffing the Ben Franklins in her braw.

"No, thank you, Peaches. You came through for us. Do you mind if we come back later and pick up the guns? We have to go hit the mall up for we can get us some fresh gear. Thug is taking us out tonight," replied Jim-Bob.

"Okay sweetie, that's fine with me. But Geno, you make sure that you keep them hoes away from Lil E, he's all mines tonight. I have enough pussy to last him his whole stay in Charlotte," said Peaches while patting her pussy with her MP5. All three men laughed at Peaches' comment then told her how much they appreciated her before leaving to go to the mall.

"Damn Ty. How the fuck did we let them niggaz get away? We had them niggaz at the red light bullshitting. And not only did we let them niggaz get away, they made me crash my Benz," said Pa-Pa while looking out the window at his now-wrecked S550 on a tow truck flatbed being towed away.

"Bra, that nigga Lil E was hitting back with some big shit letting both of his pistols roll at the same time. I had to duck while firing at the same time. But I could've sworn that I hit Jim-Bob up before he smashed off because as soon as we pulled up beside his Range I got the hitting off through his driver side window. But I'm not even going to lie, bra, I slipped and underestimated the power of the lil compact Glock 33 .357. That lil muthafucka was trying to jump out of my hands until I got a firm grip on the handle and started hitting with both hands wrapped around the handle," replied Ty.

Ty, short for Ty-Tank, was a lil short, black nigga from around Lench Mob. Ty had a vicious lil-man complex and wasn't going for nuffing. He and Pa-Pa wanted some smoke with Jim-Bob and Lil E and wasn't going to stop gunning for their heads until both of them was dead. The beef was on.

"Ty, we been doing this shit for too long for you to be fucking up. When you out to get your man, it shouldn't be no fuck up's. Get your man then get the fuck away from the scene as quick as possible. It's not no playing around in these bloody D.C. streets. It's dog-eat-dog out there and I will be damned if I let a nigga eat me alive out that bitch. So, tighten up Slim. It only takes one fuck up or one wrong move to cost you your life out there," said Pa-Pa coaching Ty.

"You right, bra. I just soaked everything up that you just said and I'm going to take heed into it all. The jewels that you just dropped on me made me open my eyes a little more, and I'm going to make sure that I bust my gun with two hands from now on from here on out instead of one," said Ty.

"As you should. But let's go hit up Today's Seafood on Alabama Avenue. I got a taste for some stuffed crab cakes and rice with a cold, triple-mixed fruit punch lemonade iced tea."

"Naw, Slim, let's go to the one that's down Eastover on the Maryland side. That joint more low key and alias." Ty knew that the whole Southside be going to the Today's Seafood on Alabama Avenue and at the current moment he didn't feel like getting into another shootout with Jim-Bob and Lil E.

"Yeah, that joint definitely tipping like shit, moe. It's too risky up there and plus all of them K-2 heads be out in front of that joint high as shit lunching. So, like you said, let's just go to the one down Eastover," replied Pa-Pa while checking his silver and black Taurus Millennium to make sure that one was locked and loaded in the head and ready to be fired.

Fifteen minutes later Ty and Pa-Pa entered the Today's Seafood down Eastover. The first thing that they noticed when they walked into the Today's Seafood was the long lines. Standing at the back of one of the lines was a sexy, thick, black female. Pa-Pa started sizing the black beauty up immediately as he took in all her beauty. He thought to himself that the female had to be 5'4", 140 pounds. "Fun size," mumbled Pa-Pa under his breath while lusting off of the female.

"Why the fuck is you over here geekin' and shit for? What's all the mumble about? Don't tell me that this whole lil situation with Pickles got you so fucked up that you talking to yourself now," said Ty while trying to figure out what Pa-Pa was just mumbling to himself about.

"Stop saying anything. I was talking about that cool lil sexy thang right there standing at the back of the line with the Off-White outfit on and the lady Air Maxs," replied Pa-Pa.

"Damn, Slim. Shawty is a lil sexy thang. And the way that ass is sitting up in that off-white shit, ohhh lorddd."

"Tell me about it. But fall back and watch me work. I'm about to go right at her. I needs her," said Pa-Pa while stepping off and walking towards the girl standing at the back of the line. When Pa-Pa reached the girl, he stood right behind her then leaned forward and whispered in her ear and said, "Hey, gor…," then was cut off by the girl's reactions.

"Hey, what the fuck is wrong with you? You don't know me to be walking all up on me whispering in my ear. That was some rude shit that you just pulled," said the girl while spinning around on her heels with quickness and retrieving a can of pepper spray from out of her Chanel handbag.

"Please don't spray me, gorgeous. I'm already blinded by your beauty. And you are absolutely right, that was rude of me, but at the same time, I'm an aggressive nigga and I felt like me whispering in your ear was the only way to get your attention," said Pa-Pa hoping that the girl took the bait.

"You could have approached me another way. You can't just be walking up on females that you don't know all whispering in their ear and shit. That's some rude, creepy shit and you almost got dealt with," said the girl while shaking her can of pepper spray in Pa-Pa's face.

"I apologize. Now can you put the can of pepper spray away so we can start all over?"

"Sure. Now, what's your name, Mr. Bold-Ass?" asked the girl while placing her pepper spray back in her Chanel handbag.

"Mr. Bold Bold Move got your attention doe didn't it? But my name is Pa-Pa. What's yours, crazy lady?"

"I see you got jokes, but my name is Angel, Pa-Pa, and I'm next up in line. I was looking over the menu to see what I'm going to get for me and my daughter, but you came over here bothering me," said Angel.

"Well Angel, you and your daughter's meals are on me. So, once you figure out what it is that y'all want to eat, let me know for I can pay for it," said Pa-Pa while pulling out a neat stack from out of his pants pocket.

After Angel placed her and her daughter's orders, Pa-Pa paid for their food then ordered his stuffed crab cakes and rice. Ty on the other hand, had already jumped in the other line and ordered his food while Pa-Pa was putting his mack down. Once everybody had gotten their food Pa-Pa and Angel exchanged numbers then went their separate ways.

CHAPTER 8

SOUTH PARK MALL, SOUTH CHARLOTTE

Geno, Jim-Bob and Lil E hit the Louis Vuitton store hard. They all copped a Louis fit with a pair of Christian Louboutins to match their outfits. Geno copped a pair of all-black Louis jeans with a silver and black Louis shirt with a pair of silver and black Christian Louboutins.

Jim-Bob copped a pair of white Louis jeans with a white and blue Louis shirt with a pair of white and blue Christian Louboutins.

Lil E, on the other hand, copped a pair of black Louis jeans with a brown Louis shirt with a pair of black and brown Christian Louboutins with a brown and black bucket hat.

After the trio hit the Louis store, Jim-Bob navigated the Altima to the Western to get he and Lil E a room.

When the trio arrived at the Western Hotel, Jim-Bob parked the Altima then told Geno and Lil E to sit tight while he went to get a room.

After paying for a master suite with double beds, Jim-Bob shot Lil E and Geno a text and told them to go ahead and bring in their bags, while he got the room. Lil E and Geno entered the Western Hotel lobby seconds later, both carrying bags in their hands. Jim-Bob flashed them the key card to the room then told them that their room was on the fifth floor.

As the trio made their way to the elevator, Geno told Jim-Bob that he already called and booked them a private section in V.I.P. at Club Onyx. Jim-Bob nodded then said, "That's what's up."

"Bob, what, you only got us one room?" asked Lil E when Jim-Bob put the key card in the door then opened it.

"Yeah bra, one room is better. This way we can gut these bitches in the same room then switch. That's why I made sure to get us a room with two beds in it. We are going to run circles around these bitches tonight, so be ready to switch and trade bitches with me," replied Jim-Bob.

Lil E went over to the Jacuzzi and started inspecting it.

"Thug, let me see the keys to the Altima. I'm going to go home and freshen up. The club opens in three hours, and we damn sure not pulling up in no Altima. I'm going to pull the G-wagon out so y'all make sure that y'all are ready. Big Geno is about to show his thugs how he living in Charlotte," said Geno while rubbing his hands together.

"Say no more. We are definitely going to be ready. And while you are out, stop by that freaky broad Peaches' house and pick up the twin Dracos for me. We are not going out clubbing without no heat," replied Jim-Bob.

"Aite thug, I can do that. And speaking of Peaches, she texted me while we was in the Louis store. She told me to pass you her number, Lil E. Where is your phone?" asked Geno.

"Right here," replied Lil E as he pulled out his phone and handed it to Geno.

After Geno programmed Peaches' number in Lil E's phone, he handed Lil E back his phone then left to go freshen up.

"Bra, please fuck that bitch for me. Fuck the brains out that pinky looking bitch," said Jim-Bob after locking the door behind Geno.

"On John I'm going to punish that pussy for the home team, so you don't have to even worry or question that, bra," replied Lil E.

"My muthafuckin' nigga," said Jim-Bob as he gave his brother some dap.

Three hours later, Geno, Jim-Bob and Lil E pulled up in the Club Onyx parking lot turning heads. They had niggaz and bitches necking trying to figure out who it was that was behind the tints of the black-on-black G-wagon bumping Young Jeezy album "I Put On for My City."

After the trio parked, they made their way to the front of the club and got in the cut line.

Geno slapped hands with a bouncer that resembled the actor Dwayne The Rock Johnson. The Dwayne The Rock Johnson look alike felt Geno slip him a nice bankroll and instead of inspecting it, he just put it in his back pocket then started wanding and fake searching, patting the trio down one by one. Once the trio was searched, the Dwayne The Rock Johnson look alike stepped to the side and let them enter the club.

While some of the females was eager to get in the club for they can find out who was the two unknown men that Geno had with him, niggaz was stuck on stupid with envy all over their faces hating. Geno, Jim-Bob, and Lil E had that shit on crushing 'em. They was Louis the fuck down and swagged the fuck out, but the black-on-black G-wagon is really what had the niggaz waiting in line faces balled up and tight.

The moment when the trio entered the club they were met by a waitress/stripper that resembled Blac Chyna. The Blac Chyna look alike introduced herself as Black Barbie then led the trio to their section in V.I.P. Not too long after the trio got settled in, a group of Club Onyx's baddest strippers and bottle girls came over with Sparkle bottles on ice. Jim-Bob, Geno, and Lil E had it all and were about to get lit. They had glow bottles of Rose Moet, Ace of Spades, Belaire Gold, and Patron.

"Got damn, these are some thick-ass bitches. Aye thug? Tell me what's more better than having a table full of champagne with some thick-ass bitches with their asses and titties out," said Jim-Bob while picking up a bottle of Ace of Spades out the bucket and popping it. Pop! The bottle sounded off sending its cork flying into the air and champagne running all over Jim-Bob's hands and fingers.

"I'm glad that you like what I set up for us my thugs, but the real party didn't even start yet. And plus, I have a lick for us that will send you and Lil E back to D.C. loaded with a space of money," said Geno.

"Oh yeah?" asked Jim-Bob.

"You fucking right. But we will discuss that later. Now go ahead and sit back and enjoy the strippers and champagne, I will be right back," replied Geno.

"Say no more," replied Jim-Bob as he put the bottle of Ace of Spades to his lips and started sipping.

Geno walked over to the DJ's booth then slapped hands with the DJ. "DJ Jelly Bean, what's up my nigga?" asked Geno over the loud music.

"You sometimes, me sometimes, us. What's up, baby boy? How you living? Talk to Jelly Bean, I talk back," replied DJ Jelly Bean. DJ Jelly Bean was an old head from out of Chattanooga, Tennessee. He, Geno, and Seth Hank Holmes met in the vent in their rooms at F.C.I. Beckley. They all shared the same vent and used to talk to each other through the vent while on lockdown. DJ Jelly Bean would always hook up his MP3 player to his speakers and play music through the vent whenever they was on lockdown, so everybody that was in their vent started calling him DJ Jelly Bean. DJ Jelly Bean agreed to his new name then told everybody that was in the vent that he was going to be a DJ once he got out and here he was in Charlotte at Club Onyx working as a DJ.

"All is well my nigga but check this out. I have my thugs Jim-Bob and Lil E from D.C. over in V.I.P. How about you give them a shoutout and put on some music that's going to make the strippers go crazy, and not them old-ass back in the day quiet storm slow jams that you used to play in the vent at F.C.I. Beckley," said Geno with laughter.

"You can't listen to that shoot 'em up, bang bang bang, young nigga shit all of your life baby boy, but you know that I got you," replied DJ Jelly Bean.

"Good looking old nigga, this is for you. You look out for me and I'll look out for you," said Geno while handing DJ Jelly Bean 10 blue-faced Ben Franklins.

"I got you baby boy. Now go ahead and go party with your homies from out of D.C.," replied DJ Jelly Bean.

"Damn moe, where you step off to? How you just going to leave me and Jim-Bob all alone with all these bitches and champagne?" asked Lil E while pouring some Moet Rose down the crack of one of the strippers' ass when Geno walked up.

"I had to tie up some loose ends but, now them loose ends are taken care of, so pass me a bottle out of one of them buckets for I can join the party and get my party on," replied Geno. After Geno popped the cork off of a bottle of Ace of Spades, he started looking around at all of the strippers to see which one was going home with him for the night. Just when Geno's eyes landed on a white stripper that had the body of a thick black girl, DJ Jelly Bean's voice came booming through the speakers.

"Alright ladies. I got two dudes from out of D.C. over in V.I.P. by the names of Jim-Bob and Lil E. I need for all of the bottle girls and strippers to report over to V.I.P. and give them a show and night that they will never forget," said DJ Jelly Bean as his voice came booming through the speakers of Club Onyx.

A few seconds later after DJ Jelly Bean made his announcement, 2 Chains' "I Love Dem Strippers" came blaring through the speakers. More strippers and bottle girls appeared in V.I.P. once that song came blaring through the speakers. It was ass and titties everywhere.

Jim-Bob had the stripper who introduced herself as Black Barbie in front of him bent over touching her ankles, shaking her ass. Jim-Bob smacked her on her right ass cheek then smacked her on the left one. Black Barbie had butterfly wings on both of her ass cheeks. As she continued to shake what her mother gave her, Jim-Bob started making it rain on her. Black Barbie got down on all fours, arched her back, then started clapping her ass while looking over her shoulder at Jim-Bob. Clap! Clap! Clap! Clap! Was all you heard as Jim-Bob started pouring champagne all over Black Barbie's ass, giving her clapping ass cheeks a champagne shower.

It seemed like the more champagne that Jim-Bob poured on Black Barbie's ass the harder she clapped. Clap! Clap! Clap! Clap! Clap! Clap! Clap! It was ass everywhere as Black Barbie clapped that muthafucka.

Lil E and Geno, on the other hand, were having themselves a freak show. They had a big-ass orgy going on right in front of them. They had the white stripper who later introduced herself as Vanilla and three other strippers who introduced themselves as Passion, Clapping Queen, and Milkshake bumping pussies and licking and slurping champagne off of each other's areolas on the V.I.P. tables.

"Thug, these bitches going wild. This shit looks like some girls-on-girls porn from an episode off of "Girls Gone Wild Rated X." I'm horny as a muthafucka and ready to fuck something. All these bitches and champagne got my hormones jumping out the gym," said Geno while feeling the effects of champagne take over his body.

"Me too thug. I was ready to fuck something the moment we stepped foot into these doors. All these thick-ass country bitches walking around in here in thongs and shit, bussing-asses phat as shit, all enticing a nigga and shit. Better yet, let's grab some of these bitches moe and take them back to the Western," said Lil E while looking at the orgy in front of him, trying to figure out which one of the strippers was going to be his sex slave and bitch for the night.

"Cool thug. I want the white bitch Vanilla. I just got to have me some of her Vanilla and that pretty lil light pink pussy. Did you see the way that she spread her pussy lips while inserting two fingers in her pussy hole while holding eye contact with me at the same time?" asked Geno.

"Naw bra, I was too busy watching shawty named Passion bump pussies with the other shawty named Milkshake. Better yet, I'm going to go ahead and pull up on Passion and see if she's trying to slide with me tonight," replied Lil E.

"Say no more. From the looks of it, it seems like Jim-Bob already fell in love with Black Barbie, so most likely that's who he's going to probably try to get to leave with him tonight. But let me go pull up on him and see what's up," said Geno. Geno walked over to Jim-Bob and put his forearm around Jim-Bob's shoulder.

"I'm happy to see that you enjoying yourself thug, but see if Black Barbie is trying to slide back to the Western with you. Me and Lil E ready to take these bitches to the Western and dick them down," said Geno while tossing a stack of loose dollar bills on Black Barbie's ass.

"Say no more, that's what it is then. I'm about to holla at her right now," replied Jim-Bob.

"No more to be said. Handle your business while I handle mines. I'm about to go put my bid in with the white bitch Vanilla. Lil E said that he's trying to fuck Passion." With that being said, Geno went to go handle his business while Jim-Bob was about to handle his.

"Aye Black Barbie, how about we take this lil show to my hotel room? It's more money to be made and I already know that you trying to see what this D.C. dick is hitting on," said Jim-Bob while getting straight to the point.

"Damn. It's just like that, huh? But I'm down. You want to see some ass, I want to see some cash, make it rain trick, make it, make it rain trick. But naw for real doe, I'm most definitely down, but first let me go freshen up in the dressing room. All that champagne that you poured on me has my body all sticky and shit," replied Black Barbie as she started picking up all of her money off the floor that Jim-Bob and Geno tossed on her while clapping her ass.

"Cool, meet me over there with my niggaz once you done. I think that they are trying to see if some of the other girls is down to go back to the hotel too."

"Okay. I'm finna go freshen up for you daddy. I will be right back. That dick is all mines," replied Black Barbie while switching away to the dressing room.

"I put my bid in with Black Barbie, she's with the move. She went to go freshen up, so it's a go on my end. What's up with Vanilla and Passion? Is they down or is they bullshitting?" asked Jim-Bob while walking up on Lil E and Geno.

"Vanilla down, but Passion bullshitting. She said that she have to go home to her man. But you already know me bra, and know that I'm not going out without a fight, so I hit her ass with the, 'Shidd, I'll be your man for tonight,'" said Lil E.

"So, what did she say after that?" asked Jim-Bob.

"She shot the Young G down, but it's cool doe. I'm just going to go fuck Peaches while y'all do y'all thing with Vanilla and Black Barbie," replied Lil E.

"Trust me thug, you won't be disappointed. Peaches is a freak. She knows how to fuck, and her head game is out of this world," boasted Geno while interjecting.

"Once again E, please punish that pussy for me bra. Please bra, please," begged Jim-Bob.

"Thug you burnt the fuck out. But here comes ole girl now. Vanilla said that her and Black Barbie are cool with each other, so they shouldn't have a problem with riding with each other. They can follow us back to Hidden Valley to drop Lil E off at Peaches' house," said Geno.

"Bet," replied Jim-Bob.

"There you are. Is you ready daddy?" asked Black Barbie.

"Yeah, I'm ready but look, you and Vanilla got to follow us to Hidden Valley to drop my brother off since y'all girl Passion is bullshitting," replied Jim-Bob.

"Where is Vanilla?" asked Geno.

"She's in the dressing room freshening up as well," said Black Barbie.

"Cool. Go wait with her while we go get the truck ready. We are going to be out front in a black-on-black G-wagon Benz truck," said Geno.

"Okay, we will be right out," replied Black Barbie.

CHAPTER 9

BAD-ASS

"I'm going to miss your lil ass moe. It seems like we was just talking about your trial date and you moving to the adult block yesterday," said Man-Head while thinking back to when he and Bad-Ass was in the hole under investigation for the stabbing of Lamont's ratting ass.

"Yeah slim, it's crazy how fast time flies by while doing time, huh? But don't be getting all emotional and shit on me. Finish helping me pack my shit and pass me my banger from out of that pillow because it's no way that I'm going across the catwalk without it," said Bad-Ass. Today was Bad-Ass's 18th birthday and his stay on the juvenile block was now over. He was on his way over to D.C. Jail to be housed on the adult block.

"You better not go over to that muthafucka bullshitting. That's the slaughterhouse, straight gladiator school. All them niggaz doing over there is pushing that knife on each other. It's a bloody massacre over 1901 right now and you better not go over there and become a victim," said Man-Head.

"On some man shit, I don't have anything to lose. Them crackers just gave me 52 years so it's best that a nigga stay out of my way because on DA CODE if a nigga get in my way I'm blowing his ass up on GP and sending him straight to the moon," said Bad-Ass while tucking his banger in his boxer briefs.

"I feel you bra, but you shouldn't even be over there that long. And plus, I'm going to send word over there for you. You know that DA MOB over that bitch mobbing heavy," said Man-Head while referring to his niggaz that's over D.C. Jail on their mob shit.

"That's all that dat nigga Savage used to talk about was DA MOB. He on that mob shit hard as shit, kill on my mother moe."

"We all on that mob shit hard. And no, we not a gang. We a family, and DA MOB is something that we built and started calling ourselves while in jail."

"But don't y'all know each other from the streets?" asked Bad-Ass.

"Yeah. We all used to hang with each other on the streets," replied Man-Head.

"Smith your escort is in R&D waiting to take you across the catwalk. Are you ready?" asked a Correctional Officer while standing in the doorway of Bad-Ass' cell and interrupting he and Man-Head's conversation.

"Give me five more minutes to holla at my manz, then I will be ready," replied Bad-Ass.

"Okay," said the Correctional Officer as he went about his business.

"It's over with slim. I guess I will see you when you come over the slaughterhouse/gladiator school as you called it," said Bad-Ass while mocking Man-Head for what he called D.C. Jail.

"Hopefully they put you on the same unit as Boo-Boo, Savage, or my nigga TS. Most likely you going to be already gone to the feds by time I get over there," replied Man-Head.

"I hope that I do, be already gone moe. I'm ready to eat me some real food. I been eating nasty-ass soy food for the past two years. I'm trying to see what's up with some fried wraps, fried mackerel patties, fried rice, and some baked mac and cheese with a cold soda to give me a nice burp," said Bad-Ass while thinking about the food that inmates cook in the microwaves in their units out the feds.

"Smith your time is up!" yelled the Correctional Officer as he stood in front of the control bubble yelling up to Bad-Ass in his cell.

"I'm gone moe. They on some geeking shit," said Bad-Ass. After Man-Head helped Bad-Ass carry his bags of property to the sally port he embraced Bad-Ass in a brotherly hug, then told Bad-Ass to keep his head up and be safe.

Jim-Bob and Geno had Black Barbie and Vanilla on all fours giving them the best back shots of their lives. The only difference was that Jim-Bob was beating Black Barbie's pussy up while Geno was balls deep in Vanilla's asshole giving her the best anal sex that she had in her life.

"Yesss, fuck this ass daddy. Give me that dick," yelled Vanilla while throwing her ass back matching Geno's strokes.

"I knew you was a freaky bitch, now shut up and take this dick," said Geno while choking Vanilla from behind.

"Oh my god, I love that kinky shit. Fuck me, fuck me," yelled Vanilla as she started moving her index and middle finger in a circular motion on her clit.

"Got damn thug. What you over there doing to that bitch? You got her over there hitting high notes while Black Barbie over here taking the dick like a champ," asked Jim-Bob while fucking away like a jackrabbit. Jim-Bob was pounding Black Barbie's pussy. He was fucking like a nigga fresh home from prison.

"Thug this bitch asshole good as shit. You got to get you

some. She loves it in the ass and plus I don't think that she will mind switching with Black Barbie," replied Geno while snatching his condom off and shooting his load all over Vanilla's ass.

"I'm down, but I can't take no more dick in my ass. The asshole is off limits for the rest of the night, so come and climb up in this pussy," said Vanilla while wiping Geno's cum off of her ass cheeks with her sock. Nasty bitch, thought Jim-Bob.

"That sounds like a good idea girl. I mean, Jim-Bob's dick is good and all, but I need for a nigga to put that shit in my life. Make me tap out. Fuck having the dick in my stomach, I need for the dick to touch my heart," said Black Barbie while reaching behind her and snatching Jim-Bob's dick out of her sloppy, soaking wet pussy.

"Your big pussy-ass will talk all of that shit after I already slutted you out, huh? You done ate my dick off of the bone then let me cum all over your face," said Jim-Bob.

"Boy stop what you doing. Don't start being disrespectful," replied Black Barbie. After switching, Jim-Bob got in his zone. He started fucking the life out of Vanilla while Geno just couldn't seem to get in his zone with Black Barbie. Damn, this bitch pussy is deep and wide as fuck, thought Geno while feeling his dick going limp and slipping out of Black Barbie's sloppy, big-ass pussy.

Across town.

Lil E and Peaches were engaged in a hot, sweaty fucking session. Lil E had Peaches' legs damn near behind her head as he fucked her missionary, thrusting himself in and out of her sweet Georgia peach.

"Oh my god, you hitting my spot. Yesss, yesss, don't stop. Give me that dick. I'm about to cum againnnn," moaned Peaches while feeling that familiar tingling sensation approaching that she loved so much. Instead of responding, Lil E just pounded away in Peaches' pussy straight D.C. style fucking her brains out.

All you heard throughout Peaches' apartment was her sweet sexy moans and her and Lil E's wet skin smacking against each other as Lil E threw his back into his strokes.

"I'm finna cum baby. Ohhh shitt, here it comessss," yelled Peaches as she started squirting all over the place and shaking. After Peaches squirted, Lil E pulled out then started eating her pussy. Lil E couldn't get enough of Peaches' sweet Georgia peach. Peaches' pussy had its own language and was making all kinds of crazy noises as Lil E licked, sucked, and slurped on it. Lil E made sure that he paid extra attention to the clit before he started stabbing the pussy hole with the tip of his tongue. Peaches was going crazy as Lil E made love to her pussy with his tongue. After a few more seconds of tracing the insides of Peaches' pussy lips, Lil E went back to the clit and started sucking and nibbling on it.

"Shit E, that feels so good. You fucking my head up. I love the way you eating me," said Peaches in between moans.

"Turn around baby and just enjoy the ride," said Lil E as his lips glistened from Peaches' sweet pussy juices. Lil E flipped Peaches over on her stomach then made her toot that ass up, face down, ass up.

The moment Peaches felt Lil E spread her ass cheeks apart then started tracing around her asshole with the tip of his tongue, she started wondering if she was in heaven or not. Lil E wasn't bullshitting. He was bringing all of his tricks that he knew about sex out the bag tonight. Lil E started repeating the same process all over again. He started stabbing Peaches' asshole with his tongue, then started sucking and licking it while reaching his arm around her and fondling her nipple.

"What are you doing to me? Ahhh, shittt, eat this ass," moaned Peaches while feeling herself on the verge of cumming again. When Peaches felt Lil E stop eating her ass and fondling her nipples, she looked back over her shoulders and said, "Why did you stop? I was finna cum again."

"Because I want to look at this big ole ass clap while I punish this pussy from the back. Now bring your ass to the edge of the bed and toot that ass back up, you know where it's going at," replied Lil E while pulling Peaches by her waist to the edge of the bed.

"You are so funny, but tell me where it's going at baby, because I have three holes," said Peaches while throwing a mean, deep arch in her back.

"You know where it's going at, it's going in your guts," said Lil E in his man Fat Todd's voice while ramming his dick in Peaches' sweet, tight, wet Georgia peach.

"Shit, I love this dick E, fuck me, fuck me," yelled Peaches while Lil E put the dick on her.

"You love this dick, huh?" SMACK! Asked Lil E while smacking Peaches on her round, phat ass.

"Yesss, I love it E. Oh my god, why are you fucking me like this? You going to make me come to D.C. and stalk you." This bitch crazy, thought Lil E as he continued to go deep in Peaches' guts.

"Harder E, harder. Make this pussy squirt again," yelled Peaches while throwing that ass back and fucking back. That was music to Lil E's ears. He placed one leg up on the bed placing his foot on the edge and did z in the pussy.

"Ahhh, I'm cumming," yelled Peaches as she squirted all over Lil E's stomach, chest, and dick. After a few more strokes, Lil E busted a nice strong nut deep in Peaches' pussy and guts, then passed out butter balled ass naked. Sweet dreams.

CHAPTER 10

IF IT'S NOT ONE THING IT'S ANOTHER

Streetz was laying on his back listening to his radio while Reckless Slim was on the floor doing sets of pushups.

"Get out that bed and come get some of this money Streetz. I know you tired of laying in bed all day," said Reckless Slim after doing another set of pushups.

"I be in my zone thinking about my mother. I'm sure she's hurt about my arrest. Mentally, physically, and emotionally Slim. She was worried about me while I was out in the streets running around like a chicken with it's head cut off. I'm talking about running straight wild out that bitch," said Streetz while thinking about the last conversation he and his mother Ms. Carolyn last had.

"Yeah, I'm sure that she's hurt and fucked up too my nigga. Besides your older brother Twione that lives in Florida you was pretty much all that she had out there in that cold world. Your father Big Todd got killed back in the '90's and that left her with just you, Savage, and Stink. Twione is all the way down Florida on a beach enjoying life with his feet kicked up drunk so it's not much that he can really do. Your mother needs y'all Slim. She's getting old and y'all are supposed to be there to take care of her and spoil her for all of the bullshit that y'all put her through. With all of y'all gone, who's going to protect her Streetz? Did you ever think about that? Mom's is strong and all, but she's tired bra. Enough is enough."

"You absolutely right Slim. I never looked at it that way, but next time they bring the phone on the range I'm going to call mom and holla at….." A Correctional Officer knocking on Streetz and Reckless Slim's cell door interrupted and cut their conversation off by telling Streetz to get ready to take a trip downtown.

"Fuck am I going downtown for C.O.?" asked Streetz.

"I'm not sure. I just got a call from the captain telling me to tell you to get yourself together you taking a trip downtown."

"Aite, give me a few seconds to get myself together. I got to wash my face and brush my teeth," replied Streetz.

"Okay, I will be back in a few minutes," said the Correctional Officer. After Streetz brushed his teeth and washed his face he slipped on his orange two-piece jail uniform with some all-white institutional Nikes from the commissary.

"Holmes, are you ready?" asked the Correctional Officer while preparing the black box and jailhouse jewelry which was a three-piece. The three-piece was leg irons, handcuffs, and a belly chain, and was what the officers used to transport inmates in.

"Yeah, I'm ready moe," replied Streetz while stepping to the door to be cuffed up. Once Streetz was cuffed up the Correctional Officer placed two fingers into his own mouth then did a loud whistle and said, "Open number eight cell."

After the Correctional Officer placed the black box and jailhouse jewelry on Streetz he was taken to R&D where he was met by the captain, major, and two first district police officers. When Streetz noticed the two first district male police officers he spoke and said, "Captain, why is the outside police here for me?" Streetz had a confused look on his face.

"Mr. Holmes, this is Officer Tate and his partner Officer Hill. Mr. Tate and Hill are officers from the first district metropolitan police department and are here to take you downtown to central cell block to be rebooked for attempted murder," said the captain.

"What the fuck is you talking about captain?" asked Streetz.

"Well Mr. Holmes, that inmate that you stabbed up in housing unit South-2 almost died. He suffered from multiple stab wounds and had to be confined to a wheelchair. Your blade on your shank that you used for this attack was very sharp and it struck the victim's spinal cord twice, leaving him paralyzed from the waist on down forever. Also, the other two guys, Mr. Henderson and Mr. Brown, who were also involved in this bloody massacre have been charged and rebooked too. Mr. Henderson was charged with second degree murder while Mr. Brown was charged with assault with a deadly weapon," replied the captain.

Damn, thought Streetz as he thought about him, Drama and Sama's knife work that they put down on Bryant and the other two unknown dudes that he was playing dominos with.

"Mr. Holmes, are you listening to me? Do you understand that y'all boys are in some deep shit? One guy lost his life while another guy is now confined to a wheelchair for the rest of his life. And the other guy is suffering from short-term memory loss from being stabbed in his head and face multiple times," said the captain.

"Cap, let's just get this shit over with. Fuck that ratting bitch and his friends. Master Splinter got what he deserved and his friends got the same treatment for playing dominos with him. If you hang with a rat, you get treated like a rat. It's smash all rats cap, and don't you never ever forget that," said Streetz not giving a fuck about Master Splinter and his friends.

"Yeah well, let's see if you're going to be talking like that when you're all the way out west somewhere in a United States penitentiary. Hill and Tate, please get this young street punk out of my presence. I'm tired of looking at his pathetic cocky ass," said the captain.

"Damn cap, be easy on the names, big guy. It sounds like you're mad because I'm a rat smasher and not a rat lover," said Streetz.

"Get his ass downtown and rebook his ass now!" yelled the captain, tired of Streetz's games and bullshit.

Bad-Ass was at the door listening to the captain and Streetz's conversation the whole time as he was waiting in R&D to be taken to his new housing unit NW-2.

"Damn Man-Head, you was right slim. These niggaz over here pushing that knife at a all-time high. It's really a bloody massacre and slaughterhouse over this bitch," said Bad-Ass talking to himself. After taking in all the information that the captain just dropped on Streetz and hearing about the stabbings that took place, Bad-Ass decided to make sure that his knife had a vicious point. Bad-Ass wet some tissue then placed it on the cell door window to block out anybody from seeing inside the holding cell.

Once the small window was completely covered and blocked off, Bad-Ass took his knife out then started sharpening it on some concrete that was in the corner on the bottom of the wall. After 10 minutes of sharpening, Bad-Ass was now satisfied with his point and ready to test it out on somebody. As Bad-Ass started removing the tissue from the window, a Correctional Officer named Taylor stopped by the holding cell and told Bad-Ass that his ID card wristband was done and that he will be taken to his unit shortly. A few minutes later Taylor returned with Bad-Ass's ID card and wristband.

After Taylor placed the jail wristband on Bad-Ass he was moved and on his way to NW-2. While walking through the hallways on the second floor, Bad-Ass ran into Block. Block was coming from medical. "Block, what the fuck is up slim? I was calling your phone all last month to thank you for the clothes and to let you know that I blew trial, but your phone kept going straight to voicemail and now I see why," said Bad-Ass.

"Sorry to hear that lil bra. Keep your head up and always remember that only the strong survive, and far as the clothes I got you for your trial, you welcome but what unit is you on?" asked Block.

"I'm on my way to NW-2. I just came over from off of the juvenile block. What unit is you on?"

"Oh okay. But I'm downstairs on SW-1 cell 46."

"Alright fellas, time is up, keep it moving," said a Correctional Officer passing by.

"I'm going to send you a kite lil bra, love you and stay sucker free," said Block as he embraced Bad-Ass in a brotherly hug.

"You already know what it is, but I love you too moe," replied Bad-Ass.

When Bad-Ass entered the sally port of housing unit NW-2 he started coughing immediately. The smell of pepper spray and blood was in the air. Yeah, I'm in the big leagues now. It smells like a straight blood bath in this bitch, thought Bad-Ass as he realized that the adult block was a big difference and much worse than the juvenile block.

As Bad-Ass made his way to his new assigned cell he looked around at his new surroundings. D.C. jail was on a half-and-half schedule, so while cells 41 through 80 were out getting their five hours of rec time, cells 1 through 40 were locked down. Yeah, I'm going to have to put my knife in one of these niggaz, thought Bad-Ass after taking in his new surroundings and stopping at his assigned cell which was cell 7. When the door of 7 cell slid open, Bad-Ass stepped into the cell and placed his property on the empty top bunk.

"What's up moe? Where you from?" asked Bad-Ass' new celly as he jumped out his bed and slid his Nike slippers on.

"I'm from around the Toga, Northeast where you from?"

asked Bad-Ass.

"I'm from around Congress Park, Southeast," replied the man.

"Oh yeah? What do they call you? I know some good men that be around the Park."

"They call me TS, short for Tuff-Slim. And who is these good men that you talking about?" asked TS.

"So you TS, huh? This a small world. I just left from off of the juvenile block with Man-Head. They call me Bad-Ass," said Bad-Ass thinking about all of the stories that Man-Head told him about TS and Boo-Boo.

"I heard of you, Bad-Ass. You the one that helped Man-Head stab up Lamont bitch ass. But anyway, what's up with Man-Head over there? Is he over there mobbing hard, cooling?"

"Yeah, that's me. We fucked that nigga up. We caught him with his dick out and put that shit up in him. And it ain't no question that Man-Head over there on his mob shit mobbing hard," boasted Bad-Ass.

After sizing TS up, Bad-Ass couldn't believe how this tall, slim nigga can be so violent, but then he also knew not to judge a book by its cover. TS was a tall, slim, light brown skinned nigga with tattoos all over his hands, arms, and neck. TS rocked his hair in a fade that everybody called a cruddy. After TS and Bad-Ass got to know each other a little more they talked about Man-Head, Savage, and Boo-Boo all the way until the 4:00 count.

Angel was going crazy as Pa-Pa continued to eat her pussy and stab her pussy hole with the tip of a nice, juicy strawberry. "That feels so good Pa-Pa, please don't stop," said Angel in between moans. Pa-Pa felt Angel's body starting to shake so he decided to place his thumb on Angel's clit, moving it in a circular motion while still stabbing her pussy hole with the tip of the frozen strawberry.

"Shit, I'm cumming," yelled Angel while cumming all over the strawberry and Pa-Pa's lips. After Angel climaxed, Pa-Pa took the cum-covered strawberry out of her pussy hole then demolished it. Angel just sat there smiling as she watched Pa-Pa eat the strawberry that had her cum and pussy juices all over it.

"Boy, you are something else, and how did I taste?" asked Angel.

"No, I'm not, I'm just a freak. And you tasted good. That was the best homemade strawberries and cream I had in my life boo."

"You are so nasty, and I guess that you do that lil trick with all of your bitches, huh? Because that damn sure didn't feel or look like it was your first time making homemade strawberries and cream Pa-Pa."

"Naw boo, that was my first time doing that. I always fantasized about doing that when I was locked up in prison," said Pa-Pa.

"Whatever boy, tell me anything, that shit did feel bomb as fuck doe. Now come and beat this pussy up. I need some dick," replied Angel as she got on all fours.

"Say no more. You not saying shit," said Pa-Pa as he got behind Angel, slamming all dick in her tight, wet pussy. The minute Angel felt Pa-Pa fill her insides up she started running towards the headboard.

"Don't run now! This what you wanted, right?" Smack! Asked Pa-Pa while smacking Angel on the ass and pinning her up against the headboard that was now crashing back and forth into the wall.

"Yes, this wh-att Iii wanted, but you going too deep in my stomach," cried Angel while feeling Pa pa's dick going deeper and deeper in her guts. Pa-Pa ignored Angel's cries as he continued to slam his dick in and out of her, fucking her brains out. After a few more strokes Angel put her big girl pants on and started fucking back and taking the dick like a big girl as she put the pussy on Pa-Pa.

"That's right, fuck back. Throw that ass back. Put this pussy on me," growled Pa-Pa while spitting on his right thumb and inserting it in Angel's back door.

"Yes, make this pussy cum again. Fuck me, Pa-Pa, fuck me. Oh yessss, fuck me!" yelled Angel. Pa-Pa stood up and squatted in the pussy while Angel was hitting high notes.

"I'mmmmm cummmming!" yelled Angel as she started shaking and cumming all over Pa-Pa's dick. Angel was a creamer and her creamy cum glistened all over Pa-Pa's dick as he slid in and out of her creamy pussy. After a few more strokes Pa-Pa pulled out then shot his thick, warm load all over Angel's ass cheeks and lower back. After Angel and Pa-Pa finished their fuck session they hit the shower then changed the bed sheets and went to sleep holding each other.

CHAPTER 11

BAT THE RAT

Today was Bat's first day back in D.C. after he testified and rocked the mic on Savage at Savage's trial. Bat went into a witness protection program somewhere in Millville, New Jersey. After being in New Jersey for over a year, Bat started getting homesick, so he decided to pack his things and go back to D.C. He was fully aware of the danger that he was in, but after selling his soul and cooperating with the law against Savage, Bat was living without a care in the world.

After Bat dropped his things off at his mother's house around 15th Place Southeast, he headed to Iverson Mall out in Temple Hills, Maryland to get some of their famous snickerdoodle cookies.

While Bat was parking his Lexus truck, he noticed Bev and Shadiamond stuffing shopping bags into the trunk of a silver four-door Jetta that was parked right next to him. "Bev and

Shadiamond, what's up with y'all?" said Bat while getting out of his Lexus truck. Shadiamond was the first one to turn her head in Bat's direction, then Bev. They couldn't believe that Bat had the audacity to speak to them after he done went and rocked the mic on their mans Savage.

"Nigga, we don't fuck with your hot ball of flame ass. Better yet, I should spit on….."

"Bev, chill girl and go ahead and go start the car up while I talk to my boo Bat," said Shadiamond while cutting Bev off and stopping her from spiting on Bat.

"Bitch, you tripping. I know you didn't just say go start the car up while you talk to your boo Bat. Please tell me that your nasty ass not fucking this nigga Shadiamond. Please, not his hot ass," fumed Bev.

"Look here bitch! I'm not going to sit here and let you disrespect me. You about to make me smack the shit out you," said Bat while getting in his feelings.

"Look, both of yall need to chill. Now Bev, please let me talk to Bat," said Shadiamond while giving Bev a look that said girl, I got this.

"Bitch, you a hot mess. If you take longer than one minute I'm leaving your ass," said Bev while walking around to the driver's side of the Jetta and getting in.

Once Shadiamond heard Bev start the car then start playing Cardi B and Megan Thee Stallion-WAP, she spoke and said, "So, Bat, where is your lil girlfriend? Y'all looked real cute together when I saw y'all at Perfect Nails Nail Salon on Alabama Avenue."

"I'm not with shawty no more. All she wanted to do is fuck, argue, and spend my money up," replied Bat.

"Well good because when I saw y'all together I wanted to snatch you away from her and put this pussy on you. You know I been crushing on you for a while now."

"Oh yeah? So, that's why you was staring at me and looking like you wanted to kill me, huh?" asked Bat.

"Yep, that's exactly why I was looking at you like that," replied

Shadiamond. Beep! Beep! Beep!

"Bat, this bitch tripping. Let me see your phone for I can program my number in it. Bev beeped the horn, so I guess my time is up," said Shadiamond.

After Shadiamond programmed her number in Bat's phone, Bat promised her that he was going to call her sometime later. With that being said, Bat made his way into Iverson Mall to get his snickerdoodle cookies while Shadiamond got into the Jetta with Bev.

"Bitch, do you mind telling me what the fuck was that all about? Like what can you and Mr. ball of flame have to talk about?' asked Bev when Shadiamond got into the passenger seat of the Jetta.

"Not a damn thing! I'm just baiting the nigga in. Shit, I might even kill this nigga myself, but first I'm going to have to put some of this bomb-ass pussy on him to get him comfortable and where I want him. This pussy is like magic, and I promise you that once I let him hit it, he's going to be gone and open for me," boasted Shadiamond.

"The killing part I agree with, but far as you fucking him, I'm against that. Like what are you going to do if Streetz finds out that you fucking the nigga that told on his brother Savage and got him behind bars?' said Bev.

"Speaking of Streetz, I tried to set up a visit to go see him when Shay set up her visit to go see Block, but when I called to make a visit, the Correctional Officer told me that Streetz couldn't receive any visits for 90 days. He's on loss of privileges and in the hole."

"Damn, that's fucked up. It seems like Streetz crew is falling apart. First, Lil Luvah got killed by the police, then Cash gets killed by the dude Menace, and now Streetz, Block, and Reckless Slim is in jail. And bitch, I know you heard about Reckless Slim lunching ass. That crazy muthafucka done went and killed two police officers. He was in the Washington Post," said Bev.

"Yeah, I saw that shit on Instagram, and far as Streetz and

Block, they should be good. Shay told me that Block said he's going to cop out to 36 months. Him and Streetz are codefendants, so Streetz should get the same cop," replied Shadiamond.

"Thirty-six months is not bad. Shit, I rather my niggaz get 36 months than 36 years on any day."

"Me too bitch. But Streetz is going to be good. I'm going to do his lil bid with him and plus I might kill this nigga Bat for him too."

"Girl, you on some Bonnie and Clyde shit, ain't you?" asked Bev.

"Something like that! But Bev, Streetz is a real nigga, and I fuck with him the long way. I'm going to be there for him and do whatever I can do to make sure that he's good in there."

"Yeah, okay. It sounds like Streetz have you sprung out and dick-matized," said Bev.

"Bitch, fuck you," replied Shadiamond while laughing at the same time.

While Bat was in line waiting to get his snickerdoodle cookies, he kept looking around at all of the people walking and shopping in the mall. His paranoia was getting the best of him, while beads of sweat covered his forehead. Bat thought after he cut his dreads off he was low key and alias.

After Bat cut his dreads, he started rocking waves and added a few pounds to his 5'9" 200-pound frame. Bat may have gained a few pounds and cut his hair, but the 1one5five millionaire medallion that hung to the center of his chest was a dead giveaway. It was finally Bat's turn to order his snickerdoodle cookies, and he ordered four pounds of snickerdoodles with a large lemonade, then high-stepped all the way back to his Lexus truck.

Once Bat made it back to his Lexus truck, he opened his bag of snickerdoodles, stuffed two in his mouth, then started his truck and pulled off.

———

Jim-Bob, Lil E, and Geno were posted outside in Grier Town on Orange Street in an all-black Charger with dark tint. Grier Town was a hood that was on the Eastside of Charlotte and was slummed out. As the trio watched crackheads and dope fiends go in and out of a trap house, Geno was telling Jim-Bob and Lil E that the trap house that they was about to hit was ran by Bloods. The two Bloods running the trap house were named Sanchez and Dave. Sanchez was a skinny, dark-skinned nigga with dreads that had three teardrop tattoos under his right eye. Dave, on the other hand, was a dark-skinned, fat nigga with plats in his hair.

As Geno ran down the lick again, Jim-Bob pulled a F&N from under his seat then cocked it, sliding one in the head. Lil E just listened carefully with one of the twin Dracos sitting on his lap as Geno ran the lick down again and again to make sure that everybody was on the same page and understood their role in the lick that was about to take place.

After Jim-Bob and Lil E told Geno that they understood and knew their role in the lick, the trio exited the Charger then made their way to the front door of the trap house. Jim-Bob and Lil E took their positions on each side of the door while Geno placed his ear against the door to see if he could hear any movement inside the trap house. Once Geno finished his safety check, he snatched a chrome and black .50 cal Desert Eagle from off of his waistline, then with no hesitation he raised his left foot then kicked the door in, sending it flying off of its hinges. Geno was the first to enter the trap house, then came Jim-Bob and Lil E. Sanchez was at the table with a neat pile of bricks sitting in front of him.

"Nigga, don't move. You know what time it is," said Jim-Bob while running over to Sanchez and placing his F&N against his temple.

"Y'all must not know who y'all…." Crack!

"Nigga, you not in no position to talk," said Jim-Bob while cracking Sanchez in the head with the butt of his F&N. Sanchez's head split open to the white meat.

"Arghhh, the money is in the hallway closet in a black trash bag," said Sanchez while wincing in pain from getting his shit split open with the butt of Jim-Bob's F&N. Blood ran down Sanchez's face and head as he winced in pain.

"Lil E, go get the money, and thug, you go check the back rooms while I sit with my new friend Sanchez here," said Jim-Bob while taking over the lick.

When Dave heard Jim-Bob say check the back rooms, he came out the back room letting his Beretta .9 millimeter do it's job. Boc! Boc! Boc! Boom! Boom! Kah! Kah! Kah! Blocka! Blocka! Blocka! Boom! Boc!

Geno, Lil E, and Jim-Bob all started shooting back at Dave with different calibers of Hydro-Shock bullets. Dave didn't stand a chance as the Hydro-Shocks entered his body then exploded, filling his fat ass up. Dave's body crashed into the floor with a loud thump. Sanchez watched the trio unload their clips on his homie from under the table where he hid to avoid being hit by a stray bullet.

"Thugs, I'm hit!" yelled Geno as he felt a burning sensation in his stomach from the two bullets that tore through his flesh from Dave's Beretta. Before Jim-Bob or Lil E could reply to Geno, he collapsed to the floor and dropped his gun.

Sanchez saw Geno collapse, so he decided to take this opportunity to try and escape, but when Jim-Bob heard his movements, he turned his F&N back on Sanchez with the quickness and shot him in the ass twice. Boom! Boom!

"Arghhhh, don't kill me man, please. I already told you where the money at, and plus you can take the 10 bricks that's sitting on the table," pleaded Sanchez while holding his bleeding, burning ass cheeks.

"Listen slim, if you can give me two good reasons why I shouldn't kill your bitch ass then maybe I will let you live and not knock your shit off, but you only got four seconds to give me your two good reasons, starting now," said Jim-Bob.

When Sanchez opened his mouth to try and give Jim-Bob two reasons for why he shouldn't kill him, Jim-Bob stuck his F&N in Sanchez's mouth and pulled the trigger three times. Boom! Boom! Boom! Blood and brains painted the walls as Jim-Bob knocked Sanchez's shit back, putting a hole that was the size of an asshole with an anal plug stuffed in it in the back of Sanchez's head.

"Bob, thug is gone slim. Let's grab the money and bricks then shake this spot," said Lil E while closing Geno's eyelids after Geno's body twitched one last time.

"Cool. You grab the bricks while I go and grab the money and finish my unfinished business that needs to be handled," replied Jim-Bob while walking towards the hallway closet to get the money. Before Jim-Bob opened the closet to retrieve the trash bag of money, he looked over at Dave's dead corpse then walked over and stood over his corpse and unloaded the rest of his clip in Dave. Boom! Boom! Boom! Boom! "That's for taking my thug with you, fat bitch," barked Jim-Bob after filling Dave's corpse up with the remaining Hydro-Shocks that were resting in the clip of his F&N.

After Jim-Bob over-killed Dave, he went into the hallway closet and started tossing stuff around until he located the trash bag full of money. Jim-Bob slung the trash bag over his shoulder then walked over to Geno's corpse and said, "Thug, I'm going to miss you slim. This shit wasn't supposed to happen like this. How did we go from clubbing and fucking bitches together to this? You wasn't supposed to get killed in your own city and on your own lick, but you know what thug? Your thug made sure that Dave's fat ass is going to have a closed casket and have to be recognized by the morgue by his teeth."

"I gave that nigga a complete makeover thug."

"Bob, thug is gone! Now let's get the fuck out of here. It's time to go back to D.C. moe. Our stay in Charlotte is now over with," said Lil E while heading out the door with the bag full of bricks.

"Yeah, you right slim. After we ditch the Charger, we can grab the Altima then go pick up our artillery from Peaches' house then shoot back to the city," said Jim-Bob while trailing behind Lil E with the trash bag full of money.

"Should we tell Peaches about Geno's death?" asked Lil E.

"Naw, let's just grab our artillery from her then get the fuck," replied Jim-Bob.

CHAPTER 12

CENTRAL CELL BLOCK

Streetz was sitting in a holding cell down central cell block waiting to get fingerprinted for the new attempted murder charge on Bryant. As Streetz sat in the holding cell waiting to be processed and fingerprinted, he thought how his life changed in just a year, and the current situation that he was now in.

Streetz's thoughts were interrupted by a dyke-looking female police officer wearing blue latex gloves. After the dyke-looking police officer opened the holding cell, she led Streetz over to a computer where she took multiple mug shots of Streetz from different angles. After Streetz was done having his mugshots taken, the dyke-looking police officer handed him a Cottonelle Wet Wipe to clean his hands and fingertips off then fingerprinted him.

Once Streetz was processed and fingerprinted, he was placed

back into the holding cell where he waited over two hours to be taken a couple of blocks over to the D.C. Superior Courthouse Criminal Division. When Streetz arrived at the Courthouse, he was taken into custody by the U.S. Marshalls. Once the U.S. Marshalls did their routine and searched Streetz, they placed him in a bullpen where he was assigned to courtroom C-10. C-10 was a courtroom that all detainees went through for arraignment court.

A lawyer came and introduced himself to Streetz as Mr. Hayes and told Streetz that he would be the one representing him in court. Mr. Hayes was in his mid-30's and looked more like a fashion model than a lawyer. Mr. Hayes' skin was as black as tar, and his 6'2" slim frame sat well in his all-black Ralph Lauren tailored suit.

"Mr. Holmes, as you may already know, you're being charged with attempted murder assault with intent to kill on a Mr. Bryant Thompson. I just wanted to let you know that most likely this case is going to go if front of Judge Lynn Leibovitz. She's the senior judge of murders and attempted murders, so most likely she's going to be the judge that this case gets handed to," said Mr. Hayes while looking through the paperwork of Streetz's jailhouse stabbing.

"I've heard about her. My homie J-Dub went in front of her for his attempted murder case. Also, I heard that she's fair with her plea offers, but if you go to trial and lose, she will drop a football number over your head plus the two-point conversion," said Streetz.

"Yeah, she's good at washing people up once they lose trial, but I'm going to need some time to go over your case Mr. Holmes, so when we go in front of the judge I'm going to have your next court date pushed back which will be your probable cause hearing."

"Okay, I'm cool with that," replied Streetz.

When Streetz and Mr. Hayes went inside courtroom C-10 a male judge by the name of Mr. Milton Lee was on the bench. Streetz and his lawyer entered a plea of not guilty, then had

Streetz's probable cause hearing set back a few months. After Judge Lee banged his gavel, he passed the case over to Judge Leibovitz just like Mr. Hayes said.

After Streetz was taken back to the bullpen by a U.S. Marshall, Mr. Hayes came by and handed Streetz his card then told Streetz that he would be over at D.C. jail to see him soon. Streets told Mr. Hayes, "Okay," then placed Mr. Hayes' card in his pocket that was attached to his orange institution shirt.

Block and Savage were going back-to-back as they were doing burpees to see who was going to get dropped off first, meaning stop first.

"Slim, this shit in me not on me. I'm a fucking machine with this workout shit. I'm built Ford tough to last nigga," said Savage while drenched in sweat and now doing two-pump burpees.

"Nigga, you not saying shit. I'm sticking with that shit. Whatever you doing I'm doing. I'm with the no-man-left-behind program," replied Block while coming up on his feet from doing a two-pump burpee as well.

"Yeah, that's right work lil bra. This whole workout thing is nuffing but a mind thing. It's a mental thing, and it's all in your mind," said Savage.

"Yeah, you right, but my shoulders are starting to burn like a mufucka," replied Block while slowing up his pace.

"That's a good thing. If it's not hurting then you not working, but we only got 40 more to do, we on 360," said Savage while trying to push Block. Instead of Block responding, he just continued to go at his own pace.

"Aye Savage, stop purping moe. You over here trying to drop Block off, don't make me burn that lil shit up," said Boo-Boo while walking over to Block and Savage, drenched in sweat from playing handball.

"Yeah, that shit sounds good, but don't watch us get money,

come and get some of this money with us," said Savage.

"Say no more," said Boo-Boo while dropping down and doing a two-pump burpee.

"I was just fucking with you slim. We about to be finished after these last few," said Savage.

"Aite, I'm just going to do the last few with y'all then," said Boo-Boo while still doing his two-pump burpees.

"What the fuck is a few burpees going to do Boo-Boo?" asked Savage while doing his last two burpees.

Block was behind five burpees, so he was still going up and down to finish his set. Once Block finished his set of burpees, Boo-Boo spoke and said, "Yeah, y'all niggaz better quit. Y'all knew what time it was." Boo-Boo was hyped up like he just did something.

"Man Block, this nigga bluffing like shit. He know damn well that he can't fuck with neither one of us on this workout shit," said Savage.

"Boo-Boo lil ass burnt out. I'm gone to the shower doe moe," said Block while grabbing his shower bag off of the floor and slinging it over his shoulder.

"Shit, me and you both. After I hit the shower I'm going to get on the phone and call Ma Dukes," said Savage.

"Y'all niggaz throwing me off, y'all jacking rec," said Boo-Boo while still trying to get his fake workout on.

"This nigga lunching good is shit. I'm gone moe," said Savage.

"Fuck y'all niggaz then. I'm already in shape and full blast anyway," said Boo-Boo while ripping out of his wife beater and showing off his lil frame.

"We love you too slim," said Savage while looking back over his shoulder.

Bad-Ass was positioned on the top left tier clutching his knife while TS was engaged in a heated argument with a dude named

Troy that owed TS $500 in commissary for some K-2 called salt and pepper.

"Listen Troy, I'm not trying to keep hearing your sorry-ass sob stories. This the third week that you missed commissary. You shouldn't had took my shit if you knew you wasn't going to be able to pay me," said TS.

"TS man, on everything that I love I got you next week. Shit just been kind of tight for me over the past three weeks, but I got you next week bra, that's my word," replied Troy.

Bad-Ass was thirsty for some action and ready to bust Troy's ass.

"Aye TS, let's bust this nigga ass and get it over with because he's playing games moe," said Bad-Ass while walking over towards Troy and TS by the shower area.

"You don't have nuffing to do with what me and TS got going on. This is between me and…." Troy's sentence was cut short as Bad-Ass pulled out his knife and started busting his ass.

TS pulled out his knife and started busting Troy as well. Bad-Ass was working Troy as he plunged his knife in and out of Troy's flesh. As Bad-Ass and TS continued to push their knives in and out of Troy, blood started squirting everywhere. Troy's body locked up, then he collapsed and fell to the floor. Bad-Ass and TS never paid no attention to Troy's cries and pleas as they both blanked out and continued to put that shit in Troy while falling on deaf ears.

A Correctional Officer saw blood splash against the plexiglass then took flight towards the shower area on the top left tier. When the Correctional Officer made it over to the bloody massacre that was taking place, he froze in his tracks as he witnessed all the blood and Bad-Ass and TS punishing Troy.

When Bad-Ass looked up and saw the Correctional Officer standing there looking all shocked, he growled then said, "Fuck 12," and turned his bloody knife on him. The Correctional Officer's eyes got big as golf balls when he heard Bad-Ass say "Fuck 12" and turn his bloody knife on him.

When Bad-Ass turned his knife on the Correctional Officer, the C.O. tried to haul ass, but Bad-Ass was all over him. The C.O. was only able to take two steps before Bad-Ass jumped on him then started forcefully plunging his knife in and out of him. The other Correctional Officer working the bubble noticed what was going on and hit the deuces.

"Cold blue, all available officers please report to NW-2. Cold blue, all available officers please report to NW-2," said a female Correctional Officer working the command center as her voice boomed through the intercom system.

The first four officers that arrived on the scene ran up on Bad-Ass then started pepper spraying him while pulling him off of their bleeding coworker. After the Correctional Officers pepper sprayed Bad-Ass and pulled him off of their bleeding coworker, they started kicking and punching on Bad-Ass. TS saw the Correctional Officers fucking Bad-Ass up, so he ran full speed towards the Correctional Officers then grabbed one of them by his shirt and started putting his knife in him. TS was only able to get five nice pokes in before he was blindsided and knocked out by a big, strong, cocky C.O.

Bad-Ass, on the other hand, was on the floor balled up in pain with his eyes burning. The Correctional Officers were still beating the shit out of him and stomping a mud hole in him. When more Correctional Officers and medical staff arrived on the scene, they never paid no attention to Troy clinging to life by the shower area. Once the medical staff spotted Troy laid out by the shower area in a pool of blood, they had to radio for more medical staff and stretchers.

In total they had two wounded Correctional Officers and two wounded inmates—one beaten to death while the other one stabbed to death. Bad-Ass was taken to medical on a stretcher right along with the two Correctional Officers that got stabbed and Troy.

When Troy, Bad-Ass, and the Correctional Officers arrived in medical, they were all air-lifted while Bad-Ass was treated in medical for his minor injuries then taken to the hole. The two C.O's and Troy were air-lifted to MedStar Washington Hospital Center. TS, on the other hand, was awakened by a cold cup of water to the face from the captain. The captain was pissed at TS and Bad-Ass for leaving a bloody massacre in his jail. In fact, this was the second bloody massacre that happened in the jail in a month.

CHAPTER 13

LENCH MOB DAY

The alley around Lench Mob was jumping and packed. Today was Lench Mob Day and the whole hood was out and turnt up while 9 Milli, a local rapper from D.C., performed.

Pa-Pa and Ty was ducked off in the corner sitting in lawn chairs with towels laying across their laps. Sitting under their towels were Mac 10 fully loaded .45's. As Pa-Pa picked up his bottle of Rose Moet, he spoke and said, "Man Ty, Milli got these bitches out here going crazy. They out this bitch clapping like shit moe."

"I see slim, but this not shit. Watch when Shy Glizzy and Big Flock get on the stage and start doing their thing and features that they got with 9 Milli. The whole hood is going to go crazy," replied Ty.

"Oh yeah. Bra got Glizzy and Big Flock coming through, that's aite right there," said Pa-Pa.

Shy Glizzy and Big Flock were two other rappers from out of D.C. Once Shy Glizzy got famous and made it in the rap industry he moved to California, but he still be moving around in D.C. here and there. Shy Glizzy was from 37th Southeast.

Big Flock on the other hand, was a rapper from out of Suitland, Maryland. Big Flock just recently touched down from doing a fed bid and was on the same compound as Seth Hank Holmes.

When Shy Glizzy and Big Flock pulled up and started performing with 9 Milli, the hood started going crazy. Bitches were going crazy as they were twerking and popping their pussies to the trio performing. Niggaz was going crazy as well. Some of them were popping bottles and pouring champagne and liquor on the bitches while they twerked and popped their pussies. Others were spraying champagne in the air giving the people that was scattered around in the crowd a champagne shower.

"Pa-Pa let's go get behind some of these bitches. I know that champagne got you on your horn dog," said Ty.

"Bra it's no question that I'm horny as shit. Better yet, I'm like a pitbull with it's lil pink thing out," replied Pa-Pa.

After Pa-Pa and Ty both stuck their Macs in their pants by the clips and handles they walked up in the crowd and got behind some ass. Pa-Pa got behind a thick, Amazon yellow bone wearing a two-piece strapless Chanel set while Ty got behind a skinny, dark-skinned, petite female that had a Coke bottle shape and an ass that was shaped like a teardrop.

After Shy Glizzy and Big Flock performed with 9 Milli, they both performed two songs apiece then wrapped it up and went their separate ways. About a minute or two after Big Flock and Shy Glizzy pulled off, two masked gunmen walked up to the crowd from out of nowhere and started unloading. Kah! Kah! Kah! Kah! Kah! Boc! Boc! Boc! Boc! Boc! One of the gunmen was letting a 100-shot Calico rock while the other gunman was letting two twin Kimber .45's rock.

Innocent bystanders were dropping left to right as the two gunmen continued to unload and chop bodies down. Bystanders were ducking, dodging, and running to avoid being hit by a stray bullet.

Pa-Pa, Ty, and a few other unknown dudes pulled out their guns and started returning shots back at the two masked gun-men. Boc! Boc! Boom! Boom! Boc! Blocka! Blocka! Boom! Boom! Boc! Shit was getting real in the alley. The gunman that was busting the two twin Kimber .45's tossed the .45's then slung a Dreco from over his shoulder then went ape shit as he started walking down on Pa-Pa and then rocking out with his cock out. Kah! Kah! Kah! Kah! Kah! Kah! Kah! Kah! Kah!

"E, what the fuck is you doing bra!" yelled Jim-Bob over the loud gun shots. By then it was already too late. Pa-Pa caught Lil E with three of his Mac 10 .45 bullets. Lil E dropped to his knees while still holding the Dreco and letting it rock out. Kah! Kah! Kah! Kah! One of Lil E's wild shots struck Ty between the eyes, killing him instantly.

Jim-Bob was still shooting it out with the other unknown dudes that were assisting Pa-Pa as he heard sirens approaching.

Lil E, on the other hand, was shit out of luck as he continued to squeeze his trigger but got nuffing but a sound that said Click! Click! Click!

Pa-Pa noticed that Lil E ran out of bullets, so he ran up on Lil E and emptied his clip in Lil E's face. Boom! Boom! Boom! Boom!

Jim-Bob watched and witnessed Pa-Pa just kill his brother and in one swift motion Jim-Bob started swinging the Calico left to right, not giving a fuck who he hit while walking backwards. Kah! Kah! Kah! Kah! Kah! Kah! After letting off a few more shots, Jim-Bob ran with the smoking Calico all the way to the car where Chuck was waiting behind tints in a dark blue G37 four-door Infinity.

When Jim-Bob made it to the Infinity then jumped in, Chuck pulled off recklessly. Boom! Boom! Boc! Boc! Boom! Pa-Pa and the other unknown dudes jumped in the middle of the street and started fucking the Infinity up as it pulled off recklessly. Boom!

Boom! Boc! Boc! Boc! The back window of the Infinity shattered into a million pieces as Pa-Pa and the unknown dudes sent shot after shot.

Jim-Bob stayed low with the empty Calico as Chuck threw the Infinity into sports mode handling it like he was Jeff Gordon. Once the Infinity disappeared down the street, Pa-Pa and the other unknown dudes ran back into the alley then jumped a fence and ran into the trap.

Shay, Bev, Shadiamond, and Meka were over at Shay's house having themselves a girl's night. Shadiamond sat on the couch with Shay rubbing Shay's stomach while she demolished a pint of cookies and cream ice cream. Bev and Meka were sitting on the floor in Indian style playing Uno while sipping on their wine glasses of pink Moscato.

"Bitch, your fat, pregnant ass just sat here and ate a whole fucking thing of ice cream and didn't even attempt to share or bother to ask any of us did we want any," said Shadiamond while grabbing her glass of wine from off the light stand next to the couch and taking a sip.

"Girl, y'all bitches better sip on that Moscato and leave me and my ice cream alone. It's two things that you never fuck with a pregnant bitch about, and that's her food and her sleep," replied Shay while licking her spoon.

"Bitch, tell me about it. When I was pregnant with baby Trevon I didn't share not a crumb of my food or snacks. I used to fuck up some cream cheese with Doritos," said Meka.

The ringing of Shadiamond's phone made Shay pause and stop licking her spoon as she said, "Friend, who is that calling your phone at this time of night?"

"Shhhh," replied Shadiamond as she put her index finger over her lips and signaled for Shay, Meka, and Bev to be quiet.

"Bitch, this is my house," mumbled Shay under her breath

as Shadiamond cut her, Bev, and Meka off then answered her phone.

"Hey Bat. I see that you good at keeping your promises. I been waiting on your call," said Shadiamond while talking to Bat. When Bev, Shay, and Meka heard Shadiamond answer her phone then said Bat's name they all looked at Shadiamond like she was crazy.

"Shadiamond, I know you not on the phone with no fucking Ba...."

"Shhhh," mouthed Shadiamond as she got up from off of the couch and went into Shay's bedroom.

"Uh uh. Y'all, this bitch is tripping," said Bev.

"Sorry Bat, them was my drunk, rude-ass friends in the backround, but tomorrow morning sounds fine to me," said Shadiamond before hanging up and setting up her breakfast date with Bat.

When Shadiamond walked back into the living room all of her friends looked and stared at her like, "Bitch, you better start explaining."

"Before any of y'all get to tripping, let me hipp y'all to what's about to go down," said Shadiamond.

"Yes, bitch! Please hipp us and put us on point because as of right now we're all ready to jump your ass," said Meka.

After Shadiamond put her girls on point and hipped them to what was about to go down, they all shook their heads then told Shadiamond to be careful. Shadiamond nodded then all of the girls went back to doing whatever it was that they were doing before Bat called Shadiamond's phone.

CHAPTER 14

Bat was sitting outside of his mother's house on 15th Place in his Lexus truck smiling. The conversation that he just had with Shadiamond on the phone left him horny as a motherfucker. All the freaky shit that Shadiamond just told him that she wanted to do to him had him geeking and ready to fuck something. As Bat laid his seat back, he fired up the half of blunt of OG that he had sitting in his ashtray. After taking a few pulls of the OG, Bat closed his eyes then envisioned how he was going to fuck Shadiamond's brains out while tossing her petite frame around.

Bat had a feeling that Shadiamond been wanting the dick when he ran into her a while back at Perfect Nails Nail Salon on Alabama Avenue. Yeah, she wants this dick. That's why the bitch was all fake mugging me when she saw me with my bitch that day at Perfect Nails, thought Bat as he leaned his seat back up then started his truck up and pulled off.

Stink was at the microwave in the dayroom doing his thing. He had the whole unit lit up and smelling good as he was making baked macaroni, fried mackerel patties, fried rice, and dumplings. Stink decided to make a meal for him and the D.C. homies that were on his unit before he got released. So, him and all of the D.C. homies on the unit all put up on the food that Stink was making.

After the microwave beeped, Stink took the mackerel patties out then started flipping them over one by one to make sure that they cook all the way through. As Stink was flipping the mackerel patties, H-Mob walked up and said, "Damn slim. You got it smelling good is a motherfucker in here. I can't wait to eat. My stomach touching my back moe, kill on Snoop."

"I got you slim. Everything is already done except these mackerel patties. The sodas and punch are sitting in a bucket under the homie table on ice," said Stink as he put the mackerel patties back in the microwave then put the timer on 15 minutes.

"Cool, say no more. I'm about to go hit this poker table up until the food gets done. Do you need anything?" asked H-Mob before stepping off.

"Naw, not really. Better yet, go ahead and go roll us up one. You already know where the smoking kit is at," replied Stink.

"Aite moe, I got you," said H-Mob as he stepped off and made his way to he and Stink's cell.

When the timer on the microwave beeped, Stink took the mackerel patties out of the microwave then yelled to the D.C. homies and said, "Aite y'all, bring me y'all bowls. The food is done!" After all of the D.C. homies brought Stink their bowls, Stink then told all of them that the cold sodas and punch was sitting in a bucket on ice under the homie table.

While Stink was making everybody's bowls, an old head from

Chi-Town that goes by the name of D$ walked up and handed Stink a homemade jail cake. "Stink, this is for you. It was a pleasure to meet you! Please be safe out there and don't come back in this shit hole! It's too much free money and good pussy out there for you to be in here with these niggaz that don't give a fuck about life or have shit to live for or lose," said D$ as he handed Stink his cake that he made for him.

"D$, it was a pleasure to meet you also. I appreciate this cake. Good looking, old head. It's finally over for me. I can't wait to get the fuck away from around all of these goofy-ass niggaz, but bring me your bowl. I'm going to put you in on this feast," said Stink.

"Good looking, Stink, but I don't eat fish lil bra."

"Well, just eat the fried rice, macaroni, and dumplings then. And plus, we got some cold sodas and punch sitting on ice," said Stink as he set his cake on top of the microwave then started loading up everybody's bowls.

"Okay, that will work. I will be right back," replied D$ as he went to go get his bowl.

Stink did his thing with the microwave-cooked food. In fact, the microwave-cooked food looked like it was cooked on a stove. Stink packed everybody's bowls to the top. He wanted to make sure that everybody went to sleep nice and full tonight.

D$ walked back up and handed Stink his bowl while Stink bit into one of the mackerel patties. After Stink loaded up D$'s bowl, he told D$ that he will bring him a soda or some punch after he finished cleaning up the microwave area. D$ nodded then told Stink that he appreciated him, then made his way back to his chair that was sitting under the sports TV.

"Aite y'all, the food is now done! I don't know which bowl belongs to who because they all look the same and wasn't marked. I filled and packed every bowl to the top then set them on the side," said Stink as he yelled to the homies and told them that the food was now done.

Once all of the homies got their bowls, they all thanked Stink then went and got their cold drinks. Stink then made his way to his cell to grab some cleaning supplies to clean up the microwave area.

When Stink walked into the cell, H-Mob spoke and said, "Slim, you're right on time. I was just about to come and get you."

"Well, now that I'm here, go ahead and put that shit in the air," said Stink while referring to the jailhouse blunt of Sour Diesel that H-Mob held in his hands.

"Say no more! Pass me a piece of tissue, foil, and them AA batteries from under my pillow," replied H-Mob. After H-Mob made the wick, he then fired up the Sour Diesel and lit the oil burner.

"Stink, I'm going to miss you moe kill," said H-Mob after he took four nice pulls of the Sour Diesel then passed it to Stink.

"I'm going to miss you too my nigga. But H-Mob, on some man shit, I got you slim. Just give me some time to get myself together." Stink took two pulls of the Sour Diesel then passed it back to H-Mob.

"I'm going to take your word because I know that you're not like a lot of them fake-ass niggaz that say that they're going to do this and that for a nigga when they touch down and hit the streets. But once they touch down and get back out there in the real world, they do shit but spin a nigga and forget about the struggle. But bra, get out there and take your time. It's no need for you to get out there and try to rush things and play catch up. Live your life and enjoy yourself my nigga. That's what life is about. Living! When you send me some pictures, I want it to be pictures of you living your best life slim, you feel me?"

"Yeah, I feel you slim, but enough said. I got you my nigga and that's ON DA CODE!" replied Stink.

After Stink and H-Mob finished smoking, Stink went to go clean the microwave area up while H-Mob went to go get his bowl of food and cold drink from off of the homie table. While Stink cleaned, H-Mob joined the homies at the homie table and started eating his meal.

CHAPTER 15

When Streetz returned back to his cell in South-1 he noticed that Reckless Slim was gone. Where the fuck this lunching nigga go, thought Streetz as he sat down on the empty bunk where Reckless Slim used to sleep. A folded piece of paper sitting on the desk caught Streetz's attention, so Streetz decided to pick up the folded piece of paper and opened it. When Streetz opened the paper, he realized that it was a kite that Reckless Slim left for him.

"Streetz, I'm gone bra. I think that I'm gone to the feds. A Correctional Officer came to the cell bland told me to pack up and that the federal Marshalls are in R&D waiting for me so they can move me. Also, I left you a banger and a bag full of food and cosmetics because I know that you're on loss of privileges. Streetz, I'm going to miss y'all niggaz. Make sure that you tell my nigga Block that I said keep his head up and walk light. Here is my

Aunt Marry's number so you can stay in contact with me—202-804-3642. Bra, make sure that you stay in contact with me too. I love you bra, and I'm forever my brother's keeper. Reckless Slim the Realest."

After Streetz read Reckless Slim's kite that he left him, Streetz programmed Reckless Slim's Aunt Marry's number in his head then flushed the kite in the toilet. Next, Streetz moved his mattress from the top bunk to the bottom bunk. After Streetz moved his mattress, he started going through the net bag full of food and cosmetics that Reckless Slim left him. The net bag was so stuffed and full that Streetz decided to dump everything in the bag out on the floor. Streetz found what he was looking for as soon as everything hit the floor.

Jackpot, thought Streetz when the banger that Reckless Slim left him slid out of an open cracker box when the cracker box hit the floor. Streetz hid the banger in his mattress then started storing his food and cosmetics into the cubbies that were attached to the cell desk. While Streetz was storing away his food and cosmetics, a Correctional Officer came to his cell door and told him that he had a legal visit and to get ready. Streetz nodded then put the blocker over the window to take a piss.

Minutes later after Streetz finished pissing the Correctional Officer came back and cuffed Streetz up then took him to-Visitation Hall-1 room 3 on the first floor. When Streetz stepped into the visitation room, his lawyer Mr. Hayes stood up, greeted Streetz with a firm handshake, then got down to business.

"Mr. Holmes, I'm going to be forward and honest with you! This attempted murder case doesn't look good for you. The inmate that you stabbed up was a witness that the government used to testify years ago on his own codefendants Mr. Hopkins and Mr. Harrison. Then on top of that, you are already fighting a tampering with a federal witness and unlawful possession of an unregistered firearm case. To me it seems like you have a vendetta for snitches, Mr. Holmes," said Mr. Hayes while looking through Streetz's case folder and paperwork.

"Actually Mr. Hayes, I do have a vendetta for snitches, and I'm going to keep smashing they ratting asses every chance that I get. Mr. Hayes, you are a lawyer, so I'm already sure that you already know how many good men are in the feds because of a snitching, ratting, dick-eating, bitch-ass nigga or bitch. I have a lot of good men plus my brothers in the feds and it's all because of a fucking snitch," said Streetz while fuming inside.

"Mr. Holmes, please calm down and listen to me. I feel your pain and understand where you're coming from 100 percent. Now listen. The government is willing to give you a plea offer of nine years of incarceration followed by five years of supervised release once you're released from prison. Also, the government is willing to run your time concurrent and give you nine years flat for the attempted murder case, tampering with a federal witness, and firearm case. This plea offer is a sweet plea, Mr. Holmes. It doesn't get any sweeter than this."

"You are absolutely right, Mr. Hayes. It doesn't get any sweeter than that. But first, I need to get in contact with my codefendant to see what's going on with him and see what was his ple…."

"Mr. Holmes, I already got in contact with Mr. Carr's lawyer Pete Daniels, and he informed me that the government gave his client a separate plea offer from you because of your new attempted murder charge," said Mr. Hayes as he cut Streetz's sentence short and updated him on what was going on with his codefendant Block.

"So, what was his plea?" asked Streetz.

"I believe that Mr. Carr took a plea to 36 months which is converted into three years followed by three years of supervised release. Mr. Carr was charged for tampering with a federal witness and unlawful possession of a firearm as well."

"Bra came off as well. It's no need to play Russian roulette with these crackers. Go ahead and get me my plea papers for I can sign my plea and get the fuck out of these people's way."

"I have all of the papers right here Mr. Holmes," said Mr. Hayes as he pulled out Streetz's plea papers from out of his suitcase then handed them over to Streetz. After Streetz read over the government's plea offer, he signed the plea then handed the plea papers back to Mr. Hayes.

"Okay, Mr. Holmes. I will get these plea papers to the government ASAP. After the plea is handled, we will just go from there. Is there anything else that I can do for you? Do you need anything?" asked Mr. Hayes while closing his suitcase.

"You're fucking right that I need something. How about you bring an ounce of OG purp and a phone the next time that you come up this bitch," said Streetz.

"The OG purp will be easy to get in, but the phone may be a little difficult to get in. I'm going to see what I can do for you doe Mr. Holmes. Now good day, I have to go," replied Mr. Hayes as he headed out the visitation room door.

Man-Head was sitting in the bullpen heated. After being in trial for three weeks fighting for his freedom, Man-Head just got found guilty on all three counts. Nay-Nay, Man-Head's wife, let a river of tears flow as soon as she heard the guilty verdict come out of the fore-person's mouth. Man-Head heard Nay-Nay's sobs and crying, so he looked back and assured her that everything was going to be okay before the U.S. Marshalls took him in the back then placed him back in the bullpen.

Man-Head's thoughts were everywhere as he thought about his wife and how hurt she was. Man-Head never thought that he would see Nay-Nay's beautiful face full of tears.

A U.S. Marshall named Toothpick stopped by the bullpen and handed Man-Head his lunch which was a stale-ass government bologna sandwich and two soggy lemon cookies. Toothpick was an old U.S. Marshall that loved to talk shit and joke with the inmates. Toothpick been working the bullpen area since the early 2000's. Toothpick also kept a toothpick in his mouth plus a fresh pack in his fifth pocket, so that's why all of the inmates that came through the bullpen area called him Toothpick.

After Toothpick handed Man-Head his lunch, he then spoke and said, "So, it's finally over, huh youngster? I been watching you come through this here system for a very long time. I'm talking about since your Youth Service Center days." Toothpick took his toothpick out of his mouth then replaced it with a new one.

"Yeah Toothpick, it's finally over. I just lost trial after fighting for my freedom and life for two years," replied Man-Head.

"Well youngster, maybe losing trial was a wake-up call for you. Do you mind me asking what was it that you lost trial to?"

"I just lost to an attempted murder charge, unlawful possession of a firearm prior conviction, and unlawful possession of unregistered ammunition," said Man-Head while looking Toothpick directly in the eyes.

"Damn youngster. I'm sorry to hear that but let me ask you this. Was it worth it?"

Man-Head thought about Toothpick's question for about a minute, then answered and said, "Toothpick, now that I have grown and learned how to handle situations in a different way and go about it a different way, no, it wasn't worth it."

"Well, I'm glad that you know that the decision you chose to make wasn't worth it. But I have other inmates to feed. Keep your head up, youngster." He walked off.

After Toothpick went about his business, Man-Head tossed his lunch in the toilet, then stretched out on the cold, steel bench and drifted off to sleep. One hour later, Man-Head was suddenly awakened by two D.C. jail Correctional Officers.

When Man-Head got back to the juvenile block, he headed straight to the phone to call Nay-Nay but couldn't get through because he had just returned from court and his phone wasn't back on yet.

"Fuck! I got to wait until after count to use the phone," said Man-Head after he realized that his phone and pack number wouldn't be back on until after the 4:00 count. As Man-Head was making his way towards his cell, a dude named Bull-Shit got on his bullshit and bumped into Man-Head while he was walking up the stairs.

Bull-Shit was coming down the stairs while Man-Head was walking up the stairs, and instead of Bull-Shit excusing himself, he did some bullshit and kept it moving. Man-Head started to tell Bull-Shit that he could have excused himself, but instead of saying something Man-Head just brushed it off and continued to make his way to his cell. If Bull-Shit really thought that Man-Head was about to let him slide, then his ass was going to learn today. He had some bullshit coming his way and wasn't even aware of it.

When Man-Head made it to his cell, he went inside the cell then wet some tissue and covered up the window for a minute or so, then removed the tissue and exited the cell. Man-Head spotted Bull-Shit on the phone with his back turned, unaware of the danger that he was now in. Man-Head walked over to Bull-Shit and got on his bullshit as well.

"You're excused, bitch," spat Man-Head while interrupting Bull-Shit's call and putting his knife in Bull-Shit's head and face. Bull-Shit called himself fighting and defending himself by wrapping his arms around Man-Head's legs and tackling him to the floor. Man-Head was locked on to Bull-Shit like a pitbull as he continued to push his knife in and out of Bull-Shit while being tackled to the floor. Bull-Shit's head, face, and back were leaking as Man-Head forcefully pushed his knife in and out of Bull-Shit's flesh.

A Correctional Officer noticed what was happening then ran over towards the bloody massacre and emptied his whole can of pepper spray on Bull-Shit and Man-Head.

"Lock down! Lock down!" yelled another Correctional Officer as he ran out of the bubble.

Man-Head flung his knife then laid flat on his stomach while coughing repeatedly and choking from the strong effects of the pepper spray. Bull-Shit on the other hand, fainted as soon as the pepper spray hit his open stab wounds and cuts. The pepper spray burnt the shit out of his skin.

CHAPTER 16

I'M MY BROTHER'S KEEPER

Jim-Bob sat in Building 1313 with Chuck drunk and high out of his mind. Jim-Bob was trying to ease his pain by smoking and drinking back-to-back. He still couldn't shake off the fact that his brother Lil E was now dead and gone. Jim-Bob couldn't believe that his brother was no longer with him. Then on top of that, he was still fucked up about his thug Geno getting killed on the lick back in Charlotte, North Carolina. Jim-Bob can still see Pa-Pa standing over Lil E and unloading his clip into Lil E's flesh and body.

"Chuck, on Fat John when I catch that nigga Pa-Pa I'm going to over-kill his bitch ass," said Jim-Bob with red bloodshot eyes.

"Bob, I feel your pain and I'm backing your play 100 percent. Whatever you with, I'm with. Oh yeah, I forgot to bring this lil situation with Angel to your attention bra. Angel be fucking with that nigga Pa-Pa. I saw them on her Instagram page all boo'd up off some lovey-dovey type shit," said Chuck.

"Whaa-whaaat, Angel?" asked Jim-Bob all fucked up and stuttering.

"Cash baby mother Angel bra. I don't know what she's doing fucking with slim, but she's definitely dead wrong! Cash haven't even been dead over a...."

Before Chuck was able to finish his sentence, Jim-Bob jumped up from off of the steps he was sitting on and shot off like a jet, knocking his Rose Moet bottle over and all.

Jim-Bob made his way straight to Angel's front door. When Jim-Bob made it to Angel's front door, he balled up his fist then started banging on the door like he was the po-po or something. Bang! Bang! Bang! Bang! Bang!

"Who the fuck is that banging on my got damn door like they're the fucking police or something? I said, who the fuck is that banging on my got damn door like they're the fucking police or something?" Angel had to repeat herself because Jim-Bob ignored her and kept banging. Bang! Bang! Bang! When Angel snatched her door open, she was met by the big barrel of Jim-Bob's Judge revolver being pointed right between her eyes.

"Whaaa-what the fuck are you doing Ji...." Punch! Angel's sentence was cut short. Jim-Bob punched Angel right in her mouth, setting her down on her ass as she fell backwards into her apartment. Jim-Bob stepped into Angel's apartment then slammed the door behind him. Angel was scared to death and ended up pissing on herself as Jim-Bob walked over to her and stood over her while placing his Judge revolver right against her temple.

"You nasty bitch. You done pissed your pants," said Jim-Bob as he noticed a big wet spot appear on the front of Angel's pants. Angel spit out a tooth as she tried to speak but couldn't.

"Look here bitch! I'm going to only ask you this question one time and you better not lie to me. If you decide to lie to me, I'm going to fuck up your pretty little face and push your shit back," said Jim-Bob as his chest heaved in and out while still holding the

Judge revolver against Angel's temple.

"What question? What is it that you want to know Jim-Bob?" asked Angel while shaking uncontrollably. She was scared to death and damn near about to shit on herself. Angel knew that Jim-Bob was intoxicated because he reeked of champagne and marijuana.

"Do you know where that nigga Pa-Pa rest his head at? If so, you better spit his address out like you just spat that tooth out over there a few seconds ago, and you only have five seconds starting now," said Jim-Bob while pointing his free hand and index finger at Angel's tooth laying on the floor.

Angel spat out Pa-Pa's address in less than 0.2 seconds. Right after Angel spilled the beans on Pa-Pa, Jim-Bob pulled the trigger twice, sending two 4.10s baby shotgun bullets crashing into the side of Angel's head. Boom! Boom! Angel's head exploded, sending brains and blood flying all over her living room.

"That's for fucking with a opp bitch!" spat Jim-Bob after sending Angel to forever live with angels. When Jim-Bob came out of Angel's apartment, Chuck was sitting on Angel's front steps cooling smoking a Newport short.

"Bob, please tell me that you didn't just kill our man Cash's baby mother," said Chuck as he flicked the butt of his Newport.

Hearing Chuck say "our man Cash's baby mother" brought Jim-Bob back to his senses. As reality kicked in, Jim-Bob realized that killing Angel was wrong. Jim-Bob wanted to take killing Angel back, but he already knew that it was too late. What was done was done! The heat of the moment just cost him to take his man's baby mother life.

When Jim-Bob just looked at Chuck with the guilty face then walked right by him, it was confirmed that Cash's baby mother Angel was now dead. It's a good thing that their daughter Samiya is over her grandparents' house because Jim-Bob probably would have killed her too if she was in the house with Angel. Do I really think that Jim-Bob will do some cold-hearted shit like that? Hell to the no! But then at the same time, there's no telling what a person will do when they're intoxicated and acting off their emotions.

Jim-Bob got into his rental car and headed to his destination on the Northeast side of D.C. When Jim-Bob arrived on 52nd and Just Street he killed the engine and waited on his prey. While Jim-Bob awaited on his prey, he reached in the backseat and grabbed a M-16 with a 50-round see through drum.

Three hours later Jim-Bob was awakened out of his sleep by an all-black conversion van bumping NBA YoungBoy's "Lonely Child" song. The driver of the conversion van parked then killed the ignition paying no mind or attention to Jim-Bob sitting behind tint of the rented Malibu.

When Pa-Pa jumped out of the conversion van, Jim-Bob tightened his grip on the M-16 then slid a 223 in it's chamber before jumping out of the Malibu.

Pa-Pa started walking towards his building then stopped when he heard footsteps approaching from behind him. As Pa-Pa turned around to see who was walking behind him, he locked eyes with the devil. Jim-Bob raised the M-16 then yelled and said, "I'm my brother's keeper!" then let the M-16 do the rest of the talking. Jim-Bob wrapped his finger around the trigger and let Pa-Pa have it. Kah! Kah! Kah! Kah! Kah! Kah!

As Pa-Pa's body hit the ground, Jim-Bob ran up and put two between Pa-Pa's eyes to make sure that he was completely dead. Kah! Kah!

After Jim-Bob completed his mission, he got back into the Malibu and pulled off. While Jim-Bob was coming across Suitland Parkway, a white 7th district police Impala with silver, red, and blue stripes that indicated the D.C. flag got behind him and hit their sirens while flashing their lights.

Jim-Bob took a quick peek into his rearview mirror then stepped on the gas pedal. It was no way that he was pulling over after committing two murders in one night. Plus, he still had both murder weapons, the Judge revolver and the M-16. Both of the murder weapons had Angel's and Pa-Pa's blood on them. As Jim-

Bob pushed the Malibu to it's limit past Anacostia Metro Station, three more police Impala cruisers joined the high-speed chase.

Jim-Bob snatched the Judge revolver off of his waistline then cracked his driver's side window and sent three 4.10's slugs crashing into the front windshield of one of the police Impala cruisers. Boom! Boom! Boom! The driver of the cruiser fishtailed then lost control of the cruiser as it flipped then burst into an inferno.

A police helicopter hovering above caught Jim-Bob's attention as he slowed the Malibu down and bucked a left turn on Nelson Place Southeast. After Jim-Bob turned on Nelson Place, he stepped back on the gas pedal bringing the Malibu to 80 MPH. As Jim-Bob was zooming through Nelson Place, he smacked the back of a Chevy Cruise pulling out of it's parking spot then lost control of the Malibu and crashed into a parked Corvette Stingray.

Officers rushed Jim-Bob by boxing him in. The strong impact from the airbag split Jim-Bob's top lip and knocked him out cold. When the officers moved in and swung Jim-Bob's driver's door open, he was knocked out unconscious with a split, busted lip.

Officers radioed for an ambulance while other officers set up the crime scene tape and blocked Nelson Place off. Once the ambulance arrived, medical staff treated Jim-Bob for his minor injuries then got out of the way. After Jim-Bob was treated for his injuries, an officer handcuffed him then read him his rights.

Nay-Nay was an emotional wreck as she sat on her loveseat crying. After calling D.C. jail to set up a visit, a Correctional Officer told her that Man-Head was back in the hole and couldn't receive any visitors. When Nay-Nay asked the C.O. why her husband was in the hole, the Correctional Officer told Nay-Nay that Man-Head was in the hole for stabbing another inmate. After the C.O. told Nay-Nay that Man-Head was back in the hole for another stabbing, Nay-Nay hung up the phone then threw it at the wall, breaking it into five different pieces.

"Fuck this shit. This nigga don't deserve a good bitch like me. I'm not fucking with his crash dummy ass no more. I am too much of a good bitch to keep fucking with a nigga that don't want to do shit with hisself but hurt people," said Nay-Nay as she got up from her loveseat and grabbed some paper and a pen then started writing Man-Head a letter. When Nay-Nay finished writing her letter to Man-Head, she went outside and put the letter in her mailbox.

After Nay-Nay put Man-Head's letter in the mailbox, she went into the bathroom and started making herself a bubble bath to calm her down and relax herself. As the tub filled up with steaming hot water and bubbles, Nay-Nay began to strip out of her clothes. Once she stripped out of her clothes, she reached under her sink and pulled out two scented peach-mango candles and a mini pink BIC lighter out of the cabinet. Nay-Nay then lit the candles and placed them on both sides of the tub, sitting them in the crack of the edges of the tub.

After she placed her candles on the edges of the tub, she grabbed her phone then scrolled through her music until she found the song that she was looking for. When Monica's "U Should've Known Better" came blaring through her iPhone 10, she climbed into the hot bubble bath and let the hot water and bubbles soothe her body.

As the bubble bath began to relax Nay-Nay's body, she spread her legs wide like an eagle then placed her right foot and leg over the ledge of the tub. She then inserted her middle finger in her pussy hole and started finger fucking herself to death. As Nay-Nay felt herself about to climax, she snatched her finger out of her pussy hole then started moving her thumb in a circular motion stimulating her clit.

Not only was Nay-Nay's pussy hot and wet, her nipples were hard and begging for some attention too, so Nay-Nay took her other hand and grabbed one of her titties and started licking, sucking, nibling, and pinching her nipples. "Ummmm," moaned

Nay-Nay as she climaxed and squirted all over her fingers and hand.

After Nay-Nay got herself off, she washed up then got in bed and watched "Love & Hip Hop Hollywood" until she fell asleep catching her some zzz's.

CHAPTER 17

NEW BEGINNINGS

As Meka's plane took off from Ronald Reagan Washington National Airport in Arlington, Virginia, she kissed her son baby Trevon on his forehead then said a quick silent prayer. After Meka said her prayer for her and baby Trevon, she started thinking about her girls Bev, Shadiamond, and Shay. Meka really didn't want to leave her girls behind, but she had to do what was best for her and her son. It was time to put D.C./ Drama City in her rearview mirror and start a new beginning. Meka had a young king to raise, and she refused to raise him around all the killing and violence in Drama City.

Meka sat in a daze as she stared out the window at the clouds thinking about how her and baby Trevon made it out. Nine hours later the captain of the plane came over the intercom and announced that the plane would be landing in five minutes and he needed for all passengers to remain seated. When the plane landed at Clearwater Airport outside of Tampa, Florida, Meka thanked God for letting her and baby Trevon have a safe trip and making it to their destination.

After the plane landed, Meka and Baby Trevon went to retrieve their luggage then called Streetz's older brother Twione that moved to Florida back in the day. Once Meka told her girls that she was taking baby Trevon and moving to Florida, Shadiamond told Streetz, and Streetz told Shadiamond that on the strength of his man's Lil Luvah, he was going to make sure that Meka and baby Trevon wanted for nuffing once they touched down in Florida.

Streetz got in contact with his big brother Twione and made it happen. Twione gave Streetz his word that he was going to make sure that Meka and baby Trevon were going to be good by any means necessary as long as he had something to do with it. Twione picked up on the first ring and told Meka that he would be at Clearwater in 20 minutes.

While Meka and baby Trevon sat around in the airport lobby waiting for Twione, Meka started looking around taking in the new scenery. The first thing that Meka noticed were the big, beautiful palm trees and lizards jumping around. Damn, it's lizards and shit jumping around down here in Florida, but in D.C. we have nuffing but fat-ass rats and big-ass possums that's damn near the size of a newborn baby running around, thought Meka as she stared out the airport's big glass window rocking baby Trevon in her arms. The ringing of Meka's phone interrupted her thoughts.

"Hello?" answered Meka while still amazed at the lizards jumping around the palm trees.

"I'm out front," said Twione as his voice boomed through Meka's phone.

"Okay, I'm coming right now. What type of car are you driving? And what do you have on?" asked Meka as she started grabbing her and baby Trevon's luggage and putting it on a cart. After Meka put her and baby Trevon's luggage on the luggage cart

Meka pushed the cart to the front exit of the airport.

"Just come out and you will see me," replied Twione.

When Meka and baby Trevon came out the airport the hot sun slightly blinded her, but she was still able to spot Twione. Twione looked like an older version of Streetz without dreads. Twione was brown-skinned with a short, stocky frame. Twione rocked a low cut with a full beard that had streaks of gray hairs in it. Twione held up a big sign that read "WELCOME TO FLOR-IDA, GOODBYE D.C." in big black letters.

When Meka noticed Twione and the sign, she smiled, waved, then started making her way towards Twione with baby Trevon still in her arms. Twione put the sign up then introduced himself. After Twione introduced himself, he went and grabbed Meka and baby Trevon's luggage from off of the luggage cart then placed the luggage in his BMW 760Li.

While Twione was placing Meka and baby Trevon's luggage in the trunk of his BMW 760Li, Meka was strapping baby Trevon into his car seat. Once baby Trevon was strapped in his car seat and the luggage was put up, Twione pulled off and navigated the 760Li to Tampa International Mall.

When Twione pulled into the huge parking lot of Tampa International Mall, he went into his pants pocket then came out with a healthy bankroll of all blue-faced hunnits and passed it to Meka. "Welcome to Florida. Go ahead and go buy whatever it is that you and your lil man need," said Twione as he handed Meka a quick 50,000 for her and baby Trevon.

"Oh my god! Twione, I cannot take th…."

"Look Meka, you and your lil man back there is now family. I gave my lil brother Streetz my word that I was going to make sure that you and your lil man want for nuffing. I told Streetz that I was going to make sure that y'all were good by any means nec-essary, and I meant it. Go ahead and go get you and your lil man some nice things while I make a quick run to go grab your keys to your new apartment," said Twione while cutting Meka off.

Meka just nodded then got out of the car and grabbed baby

Trevon from out of his car seat then made her way to the side entrance of Tampa International Mall. When she stepped into the mall, she felt like she was in a new world. Tampa International Mall was huge and had two different sides to it.

Meka's first stop was the Baby Gap. After Meka got baby Trevon 10 nice outfits from out of Baby Gap, she went into Macy's and grabbed baby Trevon 10 more outfits from out of Macy's kids section as well. Next, Meka went into Kids Foot Locker and got baby Trevon a pair of Jordans, Forces, Foamposites, Nikes, New Balance 990's, Air Maxs, and a pair of cute baby sandals.

After Meka got her son out the way and made sure that he was straight, she hit up Victoria's Secret and a few other female stores and got herself a few nice things for herself. Meka couldn't forget about Twione, so she went into Dtlr and Diesel and grabbed him two pairs of shoes and two outfits as well.

A minute or so after Meka hit up Dtlr and Diesel, Twione shot Meka a text asking her was she ready. Meka shot back and said yes, we coming now. Also, I picked you up a few things.

When Twione noticed Meka exit the mall with a shopping cart full of bags and baby Trevon, he smiled then got out of his 760 and helped Meka with her shopping bags and baby Trevon. After Meka and Twione placed the shopping bags and baby Trevon in the back seat, they pulled off and made their way to Meka and baby Trevon's new home.

Twenty minutes later Twione pulled into the driveway of a green and white two-bedroom house.

"Oh my god! Is this my house?" asked Meka as she started crying.

"Yes, this is you and your son's new home. The rest of your furniture will be delivered within the next 24 hours," said Twione as he handed Meka a set of keys that said "Home" on a keychain.

"Thank you! Thank you! Thank you!" cried Meka.

"No problem! Now let's grab you and your son's things so y'all can go check out y'all new home," replied Twione as he popped the trunk then looked in his mirror at baby Trevon sleeping. After Meka and Twione carried all of Meka and Baby Trevon's bags into Meka and baby Trevon's new home, Meka thanked Twione again then ran around her new home like a kid on Christmas.

Man-Head was sitting on his bunk reading a State VS Us magazine when a Correctional Officer stopped by his cell and slid him his mail under the door. Man-Head set the magazine down then got up and picked up his mail from off of the floor. When Man-Head noticed that his mail was from Nay-Nay, he started smiling then ripped the envelope open.

As Man-Head started reading Nay-Nay's letter, his smile instantly went from a smile to the long face while he sat back on his bunk. After Man-Head read Nay-Nay's letter twice he then grabbed a pen and some paper then started writing her back.

"Nay-Nay, I'm sorry. I know that I promised you that I was going to stay out of the hole and out of trouble, but baby, sometimes trouble just happens to find me. Baby, you really don't understand what I go through in here. Life behind these walls and bars is crazy. Life in here is kind of like life on the streets. It's a cold world behind these walls and bars. It's dog-eat-dog in here, and you have to survive in here by any means necessary. Some people come in here then never make it back home to their family and loved ones. Niggaz be out there taking penitentiary chances and throwing rocks at the penitentiary to feed their families, but when a nigga gone up the road with a number on his head, his family, girl, and loved ones no longer know him anymore. Out of sight, out of mind. Some niggaz choose to be a hard-working man with a 9-to-5 while others choose to be street niggaz and get it out the mud, staying down until they come up. Nay-Nay, have you ever seen one of your family members or loved ones walk out the door and never return? Well, it's just like that in here. Some people die or get killed in here and never make it back home. Anyways, when I got back from court, I went straight to the phone to call you but couldn't get through because my phone was off until after the 4:00 count. After that I started walking to my cell, but as I was walking to my cell a nigga bumped into me and didn't even try to excuse hisself. I don't play about my respect and that's something that I told you when we first met. Naw, I didn't have to put my knife in that nigga, but at the same time, he disrespected a man that's not with the bullshit. Nay-Nay, maybe you're right. Maybe I don't deserve you. You are definitely a good female that deserves a good man and husband, so I'm going to let you move on with your life and take this breakup on the chin. I will like to always be a friend and check on you from time to time, Nay-Nay. I love you always and forever. Love, Man-Head."

After Man-Head wrote Nay-Nay back he placed the letter in an envelope, put it in the door for a Correctional Officer to get, then started working out.

Man-Head wasn't worried about Nay-Nay not fucking with him anymore. Yes, he knew that Nay-Nay was a good bitch and all, but then at the same time he also knew that there was plenty of fish in the sea.

Man-Head started working out harder as he pushed him and Nay-Nay's breakup to the back of his head. I'm locked up, not washed up. I will be back one day, thought Man-Head as he got into a pushup position and banged out a quick 100-clip of push-ups.

CHAPTER 18

WELCOME HOME STINK

When Stink walked out of the Peter Pan Bus Station on K St Northwest in Washington D.C., his mother Ms. Carolyn ran and jumped in his arms.

"Take it easy ma. You acting like you haven't seen me in over a decade or something when it's only been three years," complained Stink as his mother put him in a bear hug, hugging the life out of him.

"Boy, you better hush up and hug your mother back! Three years is too long for a mother to go without having her child in her presence," said Ms. Carolyn as she let go of Stink.

"Well, now that I'm back home and in your presence how about we head home for I can eat my nice meal that you cooked for me. I'm hungry and lord knows that I miss my mother's cooking so, so much," replied Stink while licking his lips and rubbing his stomach.

"Okay son, let's go. I'm parked right over there," said Ms. Carolyn as she pointed across the street to a red 2017 Toyota Camry SE.

After Stink and Ms. Carolyn crossed the street, they got into the Toyota Camry then pulled off. As Stink and Ms. Carolyn were driving through the Third Street tunnel, Ms. Carolyn was updating Stink on what was going on with his brothers Savage and Streetz.

Stink was fucked up as he just sat back listening to his mother talk. He was fuming inside while his blood boiled. Stink just couldn't believe that Savage got washed up just a week ago after losing trial. Savage was just sentenced to 28 years in prison while Streetz, on the other hand, was just rebooked for attempted murder on a well-known rat in D.C./Drama City. I'm going to kill that nigga Bat's bitch ass and that's ON DA CODE, thought Stink as he zoned out and just stared at all of the cars passing by in traffic.

"Son, do you hear me talking to you? I know that look on your face and can tell that you're up to something. Don't forget that I'm the one who carried you around in my womb for nine months then gave birth to you. I know my boys well and can tell when you, Savage, or Streetz is up to something. So, with that being said, how about you go ahead and share your thoughts with your mother," said Ms. Carolyn as she realized that Stink had fallen on deaf ears and went into deep thought while she was talking to him.

"I'm sorry ma! I'm just hurt and fucked up. I mean, I'm just so messed up about this whole lil situation with my lil brothers. I never wanted to see my lil brothers go through all of the stuff that I just had to go through for three years," said Stink.

"Listen son! I know that you love your brothers and all, but you have to focus on you, your son, and getting yourself together. The judge gave you another chance to return back to society a better person and human being. Your brothers made their beds and now they have to lay in them. I worried myself to death about your lil brother Streetz running them evil streets while you and Savage was already away locked in a prison cell. I prayed that God protect my baby from all evil out here in these streets and let him return back home to me at night. The only time that boy came home is when he showered and changed his clothes or when he was being a lil whore. I had to tell that boy over and over that my got damn house is not a hotel or Motel 8. I was scared that I was going to get that call in the middle of the night saying that my son was dead, but now I don't really worry myself anymore because I rather Streetz be locked up than dead. Now, your other brother Savage, I just don't know what's gotten into him. Me or y'alls father must've dropped him on his head or something while he was a baby. That damn boy is just so damn crazy," said Ms. Carolyn as she thought about her sons Savage and Streetz in the jail system.

When Stink and Ms. Carolyn pulled up into her parking lot, Stink took a deep breath. It felt good to be back home and Stink couldn't wait to eat his nice home-cooked meal that his mother prepared for him. When he got out of the car, he stretched then said, "Damn it feels good to be home!"

After Stink stretched, he and Ms. Carolyn went into her two-bedroom apartment. Damn, Ma-Dukes went from a four-bedroom house to a two-bedroom apartment. I guess when me and Savage went away she felt like she no longer needed that four-bedroom house anymore, thought Stink as he entered his mother's small two-bedroom apartment.

"Your plate is in the oven son. I'm going to go shower then get ready to watch me some Lifetime. Welcome home son," said Ms. Carolyn as she headed into her bedroom.

Stink went straight to the oven and grabbed his nice home-cooked meal. Stink's home-cooked meal was a nice big plate of candied yams with crispy melted marshmallows on top, baked barbequed chicken breast, cheese broccoli, white rice, and baked macaroni and cheese. He also had a foil pan of homemade peach cobbler pie. Damn, Ma-dukes really threw down for me, didn't she, thought Stink as he smelled and inspected his meal and pie. After Stink inspected his meal and pie, he placed his plate in the microwave then put the timer on five minutes.

While Stink awaited on his meal to heat up, he grabbed his mother's phone off of the table then logged into his Instagram account. While scrolling down his Instagram timeline, Stink clicked on a video of Shadiamond posted up around Stanton Terrace by the Recreation Center. Shadiamond, Lot, B.Y., Bev, Jimmy Jones, Shay, and E-Doe were doing it off of Kevin. Kevin was kind of slow, but he could still function and was a funny motherfucker. Kevin was in his late 30s and usually hung in the barber shop around Savannah Terrace by Alabama Avenue, but today he was at the Recreation Center fucking around with Shadiamond and the gang.

They wild as shit all doing it off my mans Kevin and shit. And look at E-Doe, he still being a hype man and making jokes, thought Stink while watching the video of E-Doe and the gang fucking with Kevin.

After Stink finished watching the video for the third time, he jumped in Shadiamond's DM/Direct Message and sent her a message. Ten seconds later Shadiamond replied to Stink's message and told him to call her ASAP. Stink punched Shadiamond's 10 digits in and called her immediately. Shadiamond picked up and answered on the first ring.

Stink and Shadiamond talked on the phone for three minutes before Stink hung up with a huge grin on his face. After he got off the phone he went and got his plate from out of the microwave. Once Stink got his plate from out of the microwave, he cut him a piece of his peach cobbler pie then walked over to the table, sitting down and blessing his food. After Stink said his grace and blessed his food, shit got real! Stink devoured his food then went and sat on the couch and watched TV until he drifted off to sleep all nice and full.

❖ ❖ ❖

A Correctional Officer knocking on Savage's cell door woke Savage up by calling him by his last name. "Mr. Holmes? Mr. Holmes?"

"Yeah, what's up C.O.?" asked Savage with a sleepy voice.

"Holmes, federal movement. You're going to the feds. Would you like a shower?"

"Hell yeah I want a shower, and it's about time that y'all muthafuckas are moving me. Give me a few minutes to get my shower stuff ready then I will be ready," said Savage while getting out of his bunk and slipping his shower shoes on.

"Okay Holmes, just wave your hand out of the tray slot once you're ready," replied the Correctional Officer as he headed down the tier with the list of inmates that were leaving to go to the feds. The other Correctional Officer working the control bubble noticed Savage waving his hand out of the tray slot, so the C.O. hit the controls and let Savage out of his cell to shower.

"Aye, who is that in the shower? I'm about to get in the other one right next to you," said Savage as he noticed that somebody was already in the good shower that got real hot.

"This Jawbreaker, why, what's up? What, you trying to get your jaw broke or something?" asked Block while playing and trying to disguise his voice.

"Yeah aite Jawbreaker, but Block it's no need to try to disguise your voice. This 1st-N-O shit that you wrote on your shower bag tag is a dead giveaway for you," said Savage while holding Block's shower bag in the air and pointing to the words that read 1st-N-O.

"You right slim, but what's up with you? I was going to stop by your cell after I showered to tell you that I was leaving to go to the feds." By now Savage was placing his two soap dishes into the shower.

"Oh yeah? That's what's up, but I guess that means that we are both leaving because I'm gone too moe," said Savage as he stepped into the other shower and cut the water on.

"Slim, they came and got me fast as shit. It's only been three weeks since I took my plea and got sentenced," said Block.

"That's all it takes bra. Once you get sentenced and get your time you gone up the road," said Savage.

"Yeah, you're right, but let me finish washing up. I will get back with you in a few minutes," said Block.

After Block and Savage were done with their showers, they went to all the good men cells that they fucked with and told them that they were leaving to go to the feds. The Correctional Officers weren't even tripping about Savage and Block running around going from cell to cell. The Correctional Officers knew the routine when inmates were leaving to go to the feds. They go through this same routine with inmates leaving to go to the feds Monday through Friday. Inmates will go from cell to cell dropping off radios, clothes, food, knives, drugs, and all types of other stuff before saying their goodbyes.

Four hours later around 6:00 a.m. a Correctional Officer came and got Savage, Block, and a few other inmates and escorted them down to R&D to do their paperwork and changed them out of their D.C. jail clothes.

Once Block, Savage, and the few other men got to R&D they were placed into a holding cell where they waited for about an hour to be processed out of D.C. jail and handed over to the federal Marshalls and Warsaw Virginia Correctional Officers to take them to Northern Neck Regional Jail in Warsaw, Virginia where they all would get their fed register number and get designated at.

Streetz and his lawyer Mr. Hayes were back in the visitation room going over Streetz's 11-C1C plea. Streetz read over his 11-C1C plea five times to make sure that he wasn't being railroaded or getting fucked over by the government. After Streetz finished reading over his plea, he slid the plea papers and folder back across the table to Mr. Hayes.

"Mr. Holmes, I'm sure that you're satisfied with your 11-C1C plea because if you weren't you wouldn't have signed it. Am I correct?" asked Mr. Hayes while looking at Streetz's signature on the 11-C1C plea papers.

"I'm cool with the 11-C1C plea, but still I had to read over it again before I signed it to make sure that it's the same plea that we agreed to when you came to see me two weeks ago. These devils and crackers play foul ball with niggaz's freedom. They will give you a good plea, but then once sentencing day come, they try to backdoor a nigga and get the judge to give a nigga the high end of his plea," said Streetz.

"I understand Mr. Holmes! I know how the government can sometimes toss some bullshit in the game when it comes to taking a plea. Now here, take this and put it up. Please don't get caught with this," said Mr. Hayes as he passed Streetz a small balloon packed with OG purp.

Streetz immediately tucked the balloon of OG purp under his nuts as soon as Mr. Hayes handed it to him. After Streetz tucked the OG purp, he then thanked Mr. Hayes for his services and told Mr. Hayes how much that he appreciated him.

Mr. Hayes told Streetz, "No problem," then packed his suitcase and left.

Four weeks later after Streetz signed his plea he was sentenced to nine years for tampering with a federal witness, unlawful possession of an unregistered firearm, and attempted murder with assault with intent to kill.

Two weeks later after Streetz was sentenced he left to go to Northern Neck Regional Jail in Warsaw, Virginia where Streetz received his federal register number and then got designated to Federal Correctional Institution Beckley in Beckley, West Virginia.

Six months after Streetz landed at F.C.I. Beckley he was transferred to United States Penitentiary Hazelton in Bruceton Mills, West Virginia for another stabbing.

When Streetz got off the bus at U.S.P. Hazelton, he was met by Reckless Slim and Bad-Ass on the compound.

CHAPTER 19

SMASH ALL RATZ

"That's right Bat, punish this pussy. Shit, fuck this pussy, yessss," yelled Shadiamond as Bat's dick slid in and out of her hot, creamy pussy.

Shadiamond's pussy was so tight, creamy, and wet that Bat never wanted him and Shadiamond's fuck session to end. Bat fell in love with the pussy as Shadiamond tightened her vaginal muscles, making her pussy grip Bat's dick like a latex glove.

"Damn, this pussy good is shit. Your lil ass got some torch!" said Bat as his eyes rolled into the back of his head. It seemed like Shadiamond got wetter and wetter after every stroke.

"I'm about to cum. Please don't stop," moaned Shadiamond as she felt herself about to climax.

"I'm about to cum too. Cum with…," Was all that Bat was able to get out before the door of the Red Roof Inn came crashing down by a masked gunman. Boom!

"Nigga, you not about to do shit but climb out of that pussy real nice and slow and lay down on the floor facedown mutha-fuckin first," barked the masked gunman while aiming an all-black Glock 21 .45 at Bat's head.

Bat climbed out of Shadiamond's pussy at a turtle's pace. He was just about to cum and wasn't really ready to exit Shadia-mond's gates to her heaven. Not even with a big-ass .45 being pointed at the back of his head.

"Oh, you think that this shit is a game or something, huh?" Boc! The masked gunman shot Bat in his right butt cheek knock-ing a chuck out of that muthafucka.

"Fuck! Aite man, I'm getting down on the floor. Please don't kill me, I will give you whatever it is that you want," said Bat while laying down on the floor face first holding his burning, thump-ing, bleeding ass cheek.

"Your bitch ass got with the program quick after I put a hot one in that ass, didn't you?" asked the masked gunman.

By now Shadiamond was putting her clothes back on and halfway fully dressed as she said, "Shit Stink! Why couldn't you wait for a few more seconds? I was about to cum nigga."

When Bat heard Shadiamond say Stink, Bat's bitch ass let out a loud fart damn near shitting on himself because he knew that this was not a robbery. It was a soon-to-be homicide.

"Damn, Shadiamond. Why did you have to say my name? As you can see, he almost shitted on hisself. I wanted to have him thinking that this was a robbery. And to answer your question, I grew tired of listening to this nigga getting pleasure. You did a good job. Thanks for setting this ratting bitch up for me. I respect you and your gangsta. Now here, take these keys and go wait for me. It's the black 2017 Honda coupe," said Stink as he tossed Shadiamond his car keys.

"Okay, but let me wrap these sheets and stuff up because I'm sure that my DNA is all over them. You know this kittycat left her pussy juices all over," said Shadiamond.

"Hurry up, Shadiamond. I have a rat to smash," said Stink

while walking over to Bat laying face down on the floor and kicking Bat in his bleeding, burning ass cheek.

"Ouch! Stink, please man. I…."

"Shut the fuck up Master Splinter! I hate muthafuckas like you!" spat Stink while taking a hammer from out of his back pants pocket and bashing Bat in the head, smashing his ratting ass.

Stink was covered in blood as he continued to repeatedly beat Bat's head in, smashing his brains. Killer Mad Max didn't have shit on Mad Stink.

After Stink smashed Bat's head and brains, Stink turned Bat over on his back then started pistol whipping Bat until he knocked out all 32 of Bats teeth. Bat was already dead, but Stink wasn't satisfied yet. He was hurting inside and wanted Bat to feel him and his brother's pain. Stink could've tortured Bat and made him feel worse pain by killing him slowly but fuck that. Bat had to die, and he had to die quick.

Stink ran out to the car to get a toolbox and a big white bucket. When Stink opened the driver's door and popped the trunk, Shadiamond was sitting in the passenger seat listening to Lil Boosie "Retaliation" with a pink and black Cobra .380 laying on her lap.

"You too G," said Stink while closing the door and running around to the trunk to get his toolbox and bucket. An older man watched Stink's every move from out of his hotel window. The older man could see that Stink was up to no good because his clothes were covered in blood.

As Stink ran back into the hotel room with his toolbox and bucket, he could've sworn that he saw a figure in the blinds peeking at him. Probably somebody's old-ass grandmother or grandfather being nosey, thought Stink as he sat his toolbox and bucket down and started going to work on Bat's corpse.

The first thing that Stink did was grab a mini ax and chopped off Bat's dick. After he chopped off Bat's dick, he stuffed the dick into Bat's mouth then took some thread and a needle and sewed Bat's lips shut with his dick stuffed inside of his mouth. Stink made sure to only sew the sides of Bat's lips shut so Bat's dick can have enough room to hang out of his mouth. No homo.

After Stink finished sewing Bat's lips shut, he stood over Bat's corpse and said, "FREE DA MOB BITCH!" then emptied his clip into Bat's corpse, rocking the corpse left to right. Boc! Boc! Boc! Boc! Boc! Boc! Stink put his gun on his hip then picked up the big white bucket turning it upside down over Bat's corpse. Baby rats and black mamba snakes fell on top of Bat's corpse as Stink turned the bucket upside down over the top of Bat's corpse.

"You wanted to be a rat, so you died with ratz. Black mambas, eat Master Splinter and his family alive!" said Stink as the vicious baby black mambas started eating and attacking Master Splinter and his family of ratz.

When Stink exited the hotel room, he noticed that the Red Roof Inn's parking lot was surrounded by Prince Georges County Police.

What the fuck, thought Stink as he looked around at all of the Prince Georges County police officers scattered around throughout the Red Roof Inn's parking lot. There was no way that Stink was going back to jail. He hadn't even really gotten his kids out the street or really gotten his dick wet yet.

"Get down with your hands above your head," barked a white Prince Georges County police officer as his voice boomed through the bullhorn that he held in his right hand while holding a Sig .9mm in his left hand, pointing it directly at the center of Stink's chest. Stink had to make a quick decision that would either cost him his life or freedom. Fuck this shit, I'm going out like a real G holding court in the streets, thought Stink while closing his eyes.

"This is your last and final warning. Get down on your knees with your hands above your head." Boc! Boc! Boc! Boc! Stink heard the shots but didn't feel anything. When Stink opened his eyes, Shadiamond was out of the car shooting her .380 at the

Prince Georges County police officers.

"Shadiamond noooo!" yelled Stink, but it was already too late.

TO BE CONTINUED.

D.C. STREET SAVAGEZ III - FED BOUND coming soon!

DC STREET SAVAGEZ III - FED BOUND

CHAPTER 1

Boc! Boc! Boc! Boc! Officers took cover behind their police cruisers as Shadiamond fired shots from her .380 pistol at them. As officers took cover behind their police cruisers, Stink made a run to his car.

"Girl, bring your crazy ass on. Let's get the fuck out of here," said Stink as he got into the driver's seat of the Honda Accord coupe. Shadiamond fired three more shots while walking backwards to the passenger side door and jumping in. Boc! Boc! Boc!

Stink pulled off recklessly out of the Red Roof Inn parking lot as he and Shadiamond fled away from the scene. Boom! Boom! Boom! Tink! Tink! Tink! Officers fired at Stink and Shadiamond as they fled away. Tink! Tink! Tink! Was the sound that the bullets made as they crashed into the trunk and back bumper of the Honda Accord before the back window exploded.

Officers got into their police cruisers and began to pursue Stink and Shadiamond as they fled away. Stink knew from his past experience of dealing with Princes Georges County Police that he only had five minutes tops to shake them before the helicopter comes out and joins the chase. Once the helicopter comes out, that's your ass. There's no escaping!

"Shit Shadiamond! Fucking with your crazy ass done got us in a high-speed chase," said Stink as he noticed five Prince Georges County police cruisers speeding behind him and Shadiamond. As Stink continued to look through his rearview mirror, he became frustrated at all of the flashing lights and sirens blaring from the police cruisers.

"Shit Shadiamond, shit!"

"Nigga, if anything, Shadiamond just saved your black ass from either catching a hot slug from them peoples or a life sentence. Either way, they was about to put your black ass down until I started firing shots from my best bitch pinky," said Shadiamond as she kissed her pink .380 on the tip of its barrel.

About the Author

Seth Holmes was born January 21st, 1994, at D.C. General Hospital in Washington D.C. Seth is the youngest of four boys and was born and raised around One Deuce, Southeast. Seth is serving a 13-year sentence in the feds and has been a fan of urban novels since 2012, and thought that if others can do it then so could he. Seth can be reached on Instagram:@Southeast_Hank

www.ingramcontent.com/pod-product-compliance
Lightning Source LLC
Chambersburg PA
CBHW060555100726
47907CB00005B/1378